the Collector's Book-shelf Value Guide

Books by Joseph Raymond LeFontaine

The Collector's Bookshelf

A Handbook for Booklovers

Turning Paper to Gold

The International Book Collector's Directory

You Can Write Yourself a Fortune

Investor's Guide to Rare Books

Joseph Raymond LeFontaine

A Companion to *The Collector's Bookshelf*

Prometheus Books
Buffalo, New York

 Inquiries should be addressed to Prometheus Books, 700 E. Amherst Street, Buffalo, New York 14215, 716-837-2475.

94 93 92 91 90   5 4 3 2 1

The publisher and the author assume no liability, implied or otherwise, in the use of the information presented in this book. Users should be aware that book values differ widely throughout North America and Europe and are subject to the laws of supply and demand. Always keep in mind that the value of any merchandise is that which a willing buyer will pay a willing seller.

Library of Congress Catalog Card Number 90-63999

ISBN 0-87975-606-3

Printed in the United States of America on acid-free paper.

To all the authors whose works are listed in
The Collector's Bookshelf,
without them the world would be dark and grim indeed,
and this book would not be needed.

Contents

Preface

For those of you who are concerned with the value of any book listed in Section III of *The Collector's Bookshelf,* "The Authors and Their Books," I have provided this *Value Guide.*

There are estimated values for 33,614 individual book titles in this directory, written by 931 authors who used a total of 1,764 different names, including pseudonyms, or pen names. Of these 931 authors, 556 (60 percent) are American, and 375 are of other nationalities, primarily British. If you could accumulate one copy of each title listed, you would need over 2,800 feet of shelving, or over a half a mile, and the books would weigh nearly seventeen tons. If you were able to read one book each day the year 'round, it would take you 92 years to read them all. That's a lot of books and a lot of reading.

Yet this represents only a small portion of all the titles that have been published during the past 500-odd years. For the past several years, between 40 and 50 thousand new titles have been published each year in the United States. If an average of 3,000 copies of each title is printed and sold, this means between 120 and 150 million new books are printed in one year.

One of the most difficult problems that faces readers, collectors, librarians, and booksellers is locating additional information about authors and their books. When we discover an author we admire and enjoy reading, most of us want to read more. But where do we go to find the titles of other books a given author has published? Where and when were they published? If we do need this information, is it possible for us to find out which of the authors' titles are still in print and which are out of print?

There is another important piece of information that book owners should have access to. That is: How much are their books worth in the marketplace? This is particularly true for out-of-print books by authors who have become collectible and whose first editions are wanted by collectors and libraries.

This *Value Guide* is an alphabetical and numerical index to "The Authors and Their Books" section of *The Collector's Bookshelf.* It allows you to quickly locate the current (October 1990) market value of any one of the 33,000 plus book titles listed in *The Collector's Bookshelf.*

You will find an order form for *The Collector's Bookshelf* in the back of this book.

Introduction

You don't need a first edition to enjoy reading a book—usually any edition will do. But because first editions are usually of greater value than later editions, you should know how to identify them if you have any. Often they are of considerable value and knowing their value can benefit you in several ways.

This book provides coded values for the over 33,000 collectible books listed in *The Collector's Bookshelf.* The authors included are primarily novelists writing in several genres such as science fiction, westerns, the "dime novel," mysteries and detective fiction, the occult, folklore, historical romances and Gothic novels, juvenile fiction, and children's books.

The collective value today (October 1990) of all the books listed in *The Collector's Bookshelf* is over $2,268,000. If the collective value of all these books were to double in, say, ten years, they would then be worth $4,536,000.

The Values

The values in this book are, for the most part, subjective and were derived by consulting many sources from both the United States and Great Britain. For most of the titles I have included there is no prior documented history of value, and the values listed here reflect my own personal opinion as to what the fair market value ought to be. In cases where some prior documentation was located, such information was taken into account, but please keep in mind that even these values are somewhat subjective.

The primary sources for the values of collectible books are traditionally:

• book auction records and directories that compile them annually;

• book sellers' catalogs;

• directories with values compiled from book sellers' catalogs;

• shelf prices in bookstores, which range from the stores of very knowledgeable book sellers to the book sections of social service agencies such as the Salvation Army and Goodwill Industries.

The value of books is further complicated by many other factors such as condition, scarcity, popularity of the author and genre, geographic location of the seller, the general state of the economy, and the whims of the reading and collecting public.

Condition is an all-important criteria, and the value spread for a book in fine condition versus one in just fair condition can be enormous. If you want to learn more about this aspect of book collecting, I suggest you consult "Appendix A: A Reading Guide" in *The Collector's Bookshelf.*

The values in this *Value Guide* are based on the following general criteria and must be adjusted downward for any book not meeting one or more of them.

• The book is the publishers *trade* edition. Books published as limited editions, limited and signed additions, and those that have been autographed by the author will have added value.

• The book must be in very good to fine condition.

• The dust jacket must be present if the book was originally issued with one, and it must be in the same condition as the book.

• The values must be adjusted downward if the bookseller's shop is outside a major market area such as New York City, Chicago, Philadelphia, Los Angeles, San Francisco, etc. A book valued at $300 in New York City may be worth only half that amount in a smaller city or town. You must remember that the value of anything is only what a willing buyer will pay a willing seller.

• The collectibility of books may vary over a period of time as authors go in and out of favor with collectors, readers, librarians, and the general reading public.

Hardcover Versus Softcover (Paperback)

Even though paperback books have been around for a very long time—Edgar Allan Poe's *The Prose Romances of Edgar A. Poe, Etc. Uniform Serial Edition . . . No. 1 Containing The Murders in the Rue Morgue, and the Man That was Used Up*, Philadelphia, 1843, is a good example—we are all most familiar with those that appeared after World War II, often with lurid and garish cover art.

It has also become customary to produce a less expensive paperback edition of best-selling hardcover books, usually about a year after the publication of the first-edition hardcover. In these cases, of course, the paperback edition cannot be considered a first edition.

Many thousands of books, however, were originally published as paperback first editions. As a consequence, anyone wanting to assemble a complete collection of a given author's works must look for the paperbacks. For example, most of John D. MacDonald's early books were first published as paperbacks.

My point is that if you are a collector you must not ignore the shelves of used paperbacks. They can be a source of some great bargains, particularly if you find books in very good to fine condition. So, if you are looking for a particular title by a specific author—check out those paperbacks!

You can usually tell if a paperback is an original (first) edition by checking the copyright page for any previous printing history. If there is none, you are probably holding a "first." A large percentage of the books listed in *The Collector's Bookshelf* were originally published as paperbacks, and the values given in this book take that into account.

A Few More Things to Consider

Many of the authors listed in *The Collector's Bookshelf* are still living and writing. Books published after 1982 are not listed. Used books published by any given author after the last date listed should be valued at half the original cover price if they're in very good to fine condition as mentioned above.

You may notice that a high percentage of the books in *The Collector's Bookshelf* were originally published outside the United States, particularly in Great Britain. Most of these books were later published in the United States in either hardcover or paperback. If you have a title that was published in the United States and *The Collector's Bookshelf* indicates that it was first published in London, you know you do not have a true first edition. You may have the first United States edition, but that is not at all the same in terms of value. It is acceptable, however, in terms of readability or for filling out a collection (provided that your collecting interest is not specifically "first editions only"), but in these cases you should not be guided by the values in this book, which pertain only to true first editions.

If you simply want to read every book an author has written without regard to edition status and value, *The Collector's Bookshelf* provides you with a chronological checklist of each author's works.

A Final Word

No one has compiled a book like this before. I expect it to be controversial. That's all right. No one is going to agree with me on all the values of over 33,000 books by 1,764 different authors.

If you find *The Collector's Bookshelf* and this *Value Guide* useful, let me or the publisher know. There are several thousand more authors and hundreds of thousands of books still to be covered. Also, if you would like to comment on specific entries or the values for specific titles, let me hear from you. I intend to update the *Value Guide* every two years in order to accurately reflect the current market and economy. You can write to me in care of Prometheus Books, 700 E. Amherst St., Buffalo, New York 14215.

How to Use This Book

The books listed for each author in *The Collector's Bookshelf* are numbered and listed chronologically according to publication. *The Value Guide* lists these numbers and provides a dollar value for each specific title (or titles in the case of sets). Thus, book number one for an author is that author's first book, number two would be the second book, and so forth. The values are shown in U.S. dollars for each number or series of numbers. Here is an example:

Aarons, Edward S.
1 and 2. $100; 3. $85; 4 thru 9. $40; 10 thru 13. $30; 14 thru 76. $15.

This means that books number 1 and 2 are valued at $100; book 3 is valued at $85; books 4 thru 9 are valued at $40 each; etc.

Of course, this information is meaningless if you don't know what the titles represented by the numbers are. So, the actual sequence of use for this book starts with *The Collector's Bookshelf* and a specific title by any of the included authors. With *The Collector's Bookshelf* and this *Value Guide*, you have the key to savings and perhaps to making a lot of money.

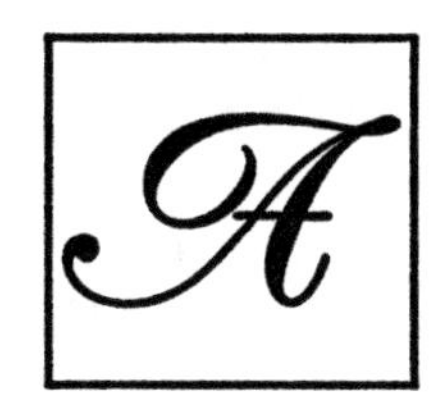

Aarons, Edward S.
1 and 2. $100; 3. $85; 4 thru 9. $40; 10 thru 13. $30; 14 thru 76. $15.

Abbey, Edward
1. $175; 2. $100; 3. $65; 4 and 5. $50; 6 and 7. $45; 8 and 9. $35; 10 thru 16. $25.

Adams, Andy
1. $375; 2. $225; 3 thru 5. $65; 6 thru 8. $45.

Adams, Cleve F.
1 and 2. $100; 3 thru 5. $85; 6 thru 8. $65; 9 thru 12. $50; 13 and 14. $35; 15. $25.

Adams, Clifton
1. $80; 2 thru 10. $50; 11 thru 15. $40; 16 thru 19. $35; 20 thru 50. $25.

Adams, Richard
1. $225; 2. $50; 3 thru 6. $35.

Adlard, Mark
1 thru 4. $25.

Agee, James
1. $540; 2. $400; 3 and 4. $375; 5. $200; 6 and 7. $65; 8 thru 13. $50.

Values shown are in U.S. dollars ($).

Ahlswede, Ann
1 and 2. $35; 3. $25.

Aiken, Joan
1. $200; 2. $125; 3. $100; 4. $75; 5. $65; 6 thru 14. $50; 15 thru 38. $40; 39 thru 52. $30; 53 thru 65. $20.

Ainsworth, Patricia
1. $65; 2 thru 6. $40; 7. $35; 8. $25.

Ainsworth, Ruth
1. $135; 2 thru 5. $85; 6 thru 44. $50; 45 thru 54. $40; 55. $35; 56 and 57. $25.

Aird, Catherine
1. $75; 2 thru 5. $50; 6 and 7. $40; 8 and 9. $30.

Albanesi, Madame
1. $300; 2 thru 13. $125; 14 thru 257. $100.

Albert, Marvin H.
1. $100; 2. $65; 3. $35; 4 thru 7. $50; 8 and 9. $45; 10 thru 20. $40; 21 thru 42. $30; 43 thru 48. $20.

Aldiss, Brian Wilson
1. $90; 2 thru 26. $50; 27 thru 46. $40; 47 thru 50. $30; 51 thru 53. $25.

Alexander, Lloyd Chudley
1. $35; 2 thru 24. $20.

Algren, Nelson
1. $525; 2. $130; 3 thru 10. $100; 11. $65; 12. $35.

Allan, Mabel Esther
1 and 2. $45; 3 thru 6. $40; 7 and 8. $35; 9 thru 13. $30; 14 thru 31. $25; 32 thru 61. $20; 62 thru 104. $15; 105 thru 133. $10.

Allbeury, Ted
1. $45; 2. $35; 3 thru 6. $25; 7 thru 9. $20; 10. $15; 11 thru 13. $10.

Allen, Grant
1. $125; 2. $85; 3 thru 9. $75; 10 thru 13. $175; 14 thru 20. $75; 21 thru 24. $175; 25 thru 26. $85; 27 thru 30. $175; 31 and 32. $85; 33 thru 39. $150; 40 and 41. $65; 42 thru 53. $150; 54. $75; 55. $65; 56 thru 59. $150; 60. $175; 61 thru 65. $65; 66 thru 68. $135; 69 and 70. $65; 71 thru 73. $135; 74. $75; 75 and 76. $125; 77. $85; 78. $125; 79 and 80. $65; 81 and 82. $125; 83 thru 85. $65; 86. $100; 87. $25.

Allen, Henry Wilson
1. $50; 2 thru 41. $20; 43 thru 49. $15; 50 thru 53. $10.

Allen, Hervey
1. $600; 2. $175; 3. $100; 4. $90; 5 and 6. $100; 7. $125; 8 thru 12. $85; 13. $100; 14. $75; 15. $65; 16 thru 19. $25.

Allingham, Margery
1. $85; 2 thru 20. $65; 21 thru 35. $50; 36 thru 42. $40; 43 thru 47. $35; 48. $25.

Almedingen, E.M.
1. $50; 2 thru 21. $35; 22 thru 71. $25; 72 thru 78. $20.

Ambler, Eric
1. $250; 2 thru 6. $135; 7. $225; 8. $75; 9 thru 15. $50; 16 thru 23. $40; 24 thru 29. $30.

Amis, Kingsley
1. $150; 2 and 3. $75; 4. $100; 5. $75; 6 thru 21. $50; 22 thru 27. $35; 28 thru 31. $25; 32 thru 34. $20.

Amy, Lacey
1. $225; 2. $100; 3 thru 35. $75; 36 thru 45. $50.

Andersen, Doris
1. $35; 2. $25; 3. $20.

Anderson, Chester
1. $35; 2 thru 4. $25; 5. $20; 6. $15.

Anderson, Colin
1 $25; 2. $15.

Anderson, Frederick Irving
1. $35; 2. $50; 3 thru 5. $25.

Anderson, James
1. $35; 2 thru 4. $25; 5 and 6. $20.

Anderson, Poul
1. $125; 2 and 3. $100; 4 thru 14. $85; 15 thru 33. $75; 34 thru 44. $60; 45 thru 53. $50; 54 thru 64. $40; 65 thru 81. $35; 82. $25; 83 thru 85. $20.

Andrew, Prudence
1. $35; 2 thru 14. $25; 15 thru 21. $20; 22. $15.

Andrews, Lucilla
1. $35; 2 thru 17. $25; 18 thru 20. $20; 21 thru 25. $15.

Angelo, Valenti
1. $100; 2 thru 8. $85; 9 thru 16. $50; 17. $35.

Anglund, Joan Walsh
1. $35; 2 thru 17. $25; 18 thru 22. $20.

Anthony, Evelyn
1 and 2. $75; 3 thru 15. $60; 16 thru 21. $50; 22 thru 29. $40; 30 thru 34. $30.

Anthony, Piers
1. $125; 2 thru 6. $75; 7. $70; 8 thru 10. $50; 11. $40; 12. $30; 13. $25.

Arbor, Jane
1 and 2. $45; 3 thru 22. $35; 23 thru 35. $25; 36 thru 54. $20; 55 and 56. $15.

Ard, William
1. $45; 2 thru 41. $35.

Ardies, Tom
1. $25; 2. $20; 3 thru 7. $10.

Ardizzone, Edward
1. $85; 2 thru 4. $65; 5 thru 10. $50; 11 thru 18. $40; 19 thru 22. $25; 23. $15.

Arlen, Michael
1 thru 4. $150; 5. $85; 6 thru 20. $35.

Armour, Richard
1. $65; 2 thru 5. $50; 6 thru 17. $40; 18 thru 29. $35; 30 thru 55. $25.

Armstrong, Charlotte
1 and 2. $50; 3 thru 5. $40; 6 thru 22. $35; 23 thru 37. $25.

Armstrong, Richard
1. $50; 2 thru 4. $35; 5 thru 35. $25.

Armstrong, William H.
1 thru 16. $25.

Arnold, Edwin L.
1. $100; 2 thru 10. $85; 11. $25; 12. $20.

Arnold, Elliott
1. $65; 2 thru 13. $45; 14 thru 19. $35; 20 thru 26. $25; 27 and 28. $20.

Arthur, Frank
1. $50; 2 thru 6. $35; 7 thru 9. $25; 10 thru 12. $20.

Arthur, Ruth
1. $35; 2 thru 6. $30; 7. $25; 8 thru 19. $20; 20 thru 27. $15.

Arthur, T.S.
1 and 2. $85; 3. $225.

Arundel, Honor
1. $40; 2 thru 7. $30; 8 thru 12. $20.

Ash, Fenton
1. $125; 2 thru 5. $95; 6 thru 10. $75.

Ashley, Bernard
1. $35; 2 thru 6. $25; 7 thru 9. $20.

Ashton, Elizabeth
1. $35; 2 thru 39. $20; 40 thru 44. $15.

Asimov, Isaac
1. $250; 2. $225; 3 thru 4. $200; 5. $160; 6 thru 9. $150 10 thru 13. $125; 14 thru 30. $100; 31 thru 34. $75; 35 thru 45. $55; 46. $75; 47 thru 53. $45.

Asprin, Robert
1. $25; 2. $20; 3 thru 6. $15.

Asquith, Nan
1 thru 8. $35; 9 thru 17. $25; 18 thru 23. $20.

Athanas, Verne
1. $25; 2 and 3. $20.

Atherton, Gertrude
1. $450; 2. $225; 3 thru 14. $150; 15 thru 37. $125; 38 thru 47. $100; 48. $85; 49. $65; 50. $50; 51. $35.

Atkins, John
1. $50; 2 thru 5. $45; 6 thru 14. $30; 15 thru 17. $25.

Atkinson, M.E.
1. $100; 2 thru 20. $75; 21 thru 30. $50; 31. $35.

Atwater, Richard
1. $65; 2. $45; 3. $30.

Audemars, Pierre
1. $85; 2 thru 8. $60; 9 thru 24. $35; 25 thru 34. $25.

Austin, Mary
1. $150; 2. $125; 3 thru 18. $100; 19 thru 27. $85; 28. $6,750; 29 thru 34. $65; 35 thru 37. $50; 38. $35; 39. $25.

Avallone, Michael
1. $50; 2 and 3. $45; 4 thru 6. $40; 7. $35; 8 thru 79. $30; 80 thru 104. $20; 105 thru 142. $10.

Averill, Esther
1. $50; 2 thru 7. $35; 8 thru 21. $25; 22 and 23. $20.

Avery, Gillian
1. $25; 2 thru 21. $20.

Ayer, Jacqueline
1. $35; 2 and 3. $25; 4 and 5. $20.

Ayres, Ruby M.
1. $50; 2 thru 132. $35; 133 thru 151. $25.

Babson, Marian
1. $35; 2 thru 13. $25.

Bagley, Desmond
1. $50; 2 thru 8. $35; 9 and 10. $25; 11 thru 13. $20.

Bailey, H.C.
1. $100; 2 thru 12. $85; 13 thru 23. $75; 24 thru 38. $65; 39 thru 73. $50; 74 thru 80. $40.

Baldwin, Faith
1. $65; 2 thru 69. $50; 70 thru 85. $35; 86 thru 104. $25.

Baldwin, Gordon C.
1 and 2. $35; 3 thru 30. $25.

Ball, John
1. $35; 2 thru 4. $25; 5 thru 12. $20; 13 thru 20. $15; 21 thru 23. $10.

Ballard, Willis Todhunter
1. $100; 2 thru 36. $85; 37 thru 60. $65; 61. $50; 62 thru 71. $45; 72 thru 77. $35; 78 and 79. $25.

Ballinger, Bill S.
1. $65; 2 thru 15. $50; 16 thru 24. $45; 25. $35; 26 thru 28. $30; 29. $25; 30 thru 34. $20.

Balmer, Edwin
1 and 2. $85; 3 thru 8. $65; 9 thru 16. $55; 17 thru 22. $50; 23. $40; 24 thru 26. $25.

Barclay, Florence L.
1. $135; 2 thru 15. $85.

Barcynska, Countess
1 and 2. $65; 3 and 4. $50; 5 thru 106. $40; 107 thru 148. $30.

Barker, S. Omar
1. $100; 2. $65; 3. $45; 4 and 5. $35; 6 thru 11. $25; 12 thru 17. $20.

Barrie, Susan
1. $45; 2 thru 40. $35; 41 thru 53. $25; 54 thru 61. $20.

Barry, Jane
1. $35; 2. $25; 3 thru 6. $20.

Bawden, Nina
1 and 2. $35; 3 thru 21. $25; 22 thru 32. $20.

Baxt, George
1. $35; 2 thru 7. $25.

Beach, Rex
1. $125; 2. $90; 3. $65; 4 thru 15. $45; 16 thru 30. $35; 31 thru 39. $25; 40. $20.

Beagle, Peter S.
1. $90; 2. $25.

Bean, Amelia
1 and 2. $40; 3. $30; 4. $25.

Beaty, Betty
1 and 2. $35; 3 thru 12. $25; 13 thru 20. $20; 21 thru 24. $15.

Beauclerk, Helen
1. $45; 2. $35; 3 thru 6. $20; 7. $15.

Bechdolt, Frederick R.
1. $225; 2 thru 4. $100; 5. $85; 6 thru 8. $75; 9 thru 14. $60; 15. $35.

Bechko, P.A.
1 and 2. $25; 3 thru 5. $20; 6 thru 8. $15.

Beck, L. Adams
1 thru 3. $65; 4 thru 38. $50.

Behn, Noel
1. $35; 2. $25; 3. $15.

Bell, Eric Temple
1. $85; 2 thru 4. $65; 5 thru 18. $50; 19 thru 21. $35; 22. $30; 23 thru 25. $25; 26 and 27. $20; 28 and 29. $15.

Bell, Josephine
1 and 2. $50; 3 thru 12. $40; 13 thru 54. $35; 55 thru 70. $25.

Bellah, James Warner
1. $100; 2 thru 10. $85; 11. $75; 12 and 13. $65; 14. $50; 15 thru 22. $35; 23. $50; 24 thru 26. $25.

Bellairs, George
1. $65; 2 thru 11. $50; 12 thru 36. $35; 37 thru 52. $25; 53 thru 59. $20.

Bellem, Robert Leslie
1. $50; 2 and 3. $35; 4. $25; 5. $20.

Benet, Stephen Vincent
1. $275; 2. $300; 3. $100; 4 and 5. $150.

Bennett, Margot
1. $40; 2 and 3. $30; 4 thru 7. $25; 8. $20; 9 thru 11. $15.

Bennetts, Pamela
1 thru 4. $35; 5 thru 34. $25; 35 thru 38. $20; 39 thru 44. $15.

Benson, Ben
1. $65; 2 thru 20. $35.

Benson, E.F.
1 thru 3. $150; 4 thru 62. $125; 63 thru 115. $100; 116. $35.

Bentley, E.C.
1. $125; 2 and 3. $275; 4 and 5. $40; 6. $175; 7. $145; 8 and 9. $40; 10. $125; 11. $65; 12. $40; 13. $35.

Bentley, Nicolas
1. $225; 2. $175; 3 and 4. $165; 5 thru 8. $125; 9. $85; 10 thru 15. $75; 16 thru 21. $50; 22 and 23. $35.

Bentley, Phyliss
1 and 2. $65; 3 thru 19. $50; 20 thru 31. $35; 32 thru 46. $25; 47 thru 49. $20.

Benton, Kenneth
1. $25; 2 thru 10. $20.

Berckman, Evelyn
1. $50; 2 thru 8. $35; 9 thru 21. $30; 22 thru 37. $25.

Beresford, Elisabeth
1. $35; 2 thru 50. $25; 51. $40; 52 thru 79. $20.

Berger, Thomas
1. $65; 2 and 3. $50; 4 thru 9. $35; 10 thru 12. $25.

Bergman, Andrew
1. $25; 2 and 3. $15.

Berry, Don
1. $65; 2. $50; 3 and 4. $35; 5. $50.

Bevan, Gloria
1 and 2. $25; 3 thru 16. $20; 17 and 18. $15.

Bickham, Jack M.
1. $45; 2 thru 10. $35; 11 thru 26. $25; 27 thru 44. $20; 45 thru 53. $15; 54 and 55. $10.

Biggers, Earl Derr
1. $85; 2 thru 13. $65.

Bindloss, Harold
1. $235; 2 thru 28. $175; 29 thru 65. $150; 66 thru 105. $125; 106 thru 130. $100; 131. $65.

Bingham, John
1. $45; 2 thru 10. $30; 11 and 12. $25; 13 thru 16. $20; 17 and 18. $15; 19 thru 21. $10.

Bingley, David
1 and 2. $45; 3 thru 82. $30; 83 thru 107. $25; 108 thru 118. $20; 119 thru 124. $15; 125 thru 127. $10.

Birney, Hoffman
1. $65; 2 thru 25. $45; 26. $25.

Black, Laura
1. $20; 2 thru 4. $15; 5. $10.

Blackburn, John
1 and 2. $45; 3 thru 19. $35; 20 thru 24. $25; 25 thru 28. $20; 29 and 30. $15.

Blackmore, Jane
1. $35; 2 thru 39. $25; 40 thru 55. $20; 56 and 57. $15.

Blackwood, Algernon
1. $225; 2 and 3. $185; 4 thru 17. $165; 18 thru 20. $125; 21 thru 34. $75; 35 thru 42. $60; 43. $50; 44 thru 49. $35.

Blake, Forrester
1. $45; 2 thru 4. $25; 5. $20.

Blake, Stephanie
1 thru 3. $25; 4 thru 6. $15; 7 and 8. $10.

Blanc, Suzzane
1. $35; 2. $25; 3. $20; 4. $15.

Bloch, Robert
1. $225; 2 thru 42. $150; 43. $75; 44 thru 49. $125.

Blochman, Lawrence G.
1. $45; 2 thru 5. $35; 6. $45; 7. $35; 8 thru 13. $20; 14 thru 25. $15.

Block, Lawrence
1 thru 3. $35; 4 thru 17. $25; 18 thru 32. $20.

Bloom, Ursula
1 and 2. $125; 3 and 4. $100; 5 thru 17. $65; 18 thru 115. $50; 116 thru 145. $45; 146 thru 232. $40; 233 thru 335. $35; 336 thru 389. $25; 390 thru 402. $20.

Bodkin, M. M'Donnell
1. $225; 2. $175; 3 thru 8. $150; 9 thru 15. $125; 16 thru 18. $100; 19 thru 23. $85; 24 thru 27. $75; 28. $65; 29 and 30. $50; 31 thru 35. $40.

Boland, John
1. $35; 2 thru 27. $25; 28 thru 32. $20; 33 and 34. $15.

Bonham, Frank
1. $45; 2 thru 15. $35; 16 thru 34. $25; 35 thru 45. $20; 46 thru 48. $15.

Booth, Edwin
1 and 2. $25; 3 thru 34. $20; 35 thru 46. $15.

Borg, Jack
1 and 2. $25; 3 thru 56. $20; 57 thru 63. $15.

Borgenicht, Miriam
1. $45; 2 and 3. $35; 4 thru 7. $25; 8 thru 10. $20.

Borland, Hal
1. $65; 2. $50; 3 thru 10. $40; 11 thru 26. $30; 27 thru 32. $25; 33 thru 36. $20.

Bosworth, Allan R.
1 and 2. $35; 3 thru 10. $25; 11 thru 14. $20; 15 thru 22. $15.

Boucher, Anthony
1. $65; 2. $50; 3 thru 7. $45; 8 thru 12. $35; 13 thru 15. $25.

Bouma, J.L.
1. $35; 2 thru 6. $30; 7. $25; 8 thru 14. $20.

Bowen, Marjorie
1. $125; 2 thru 29. $85; 30 thru 52. $75; 53 thru 103. $65; 104 thru 120. $50; 121 thru 126. $35; 127 thru 130. $25; 131 thru 134. $20.

Bower, B.M.
1. $235; 2 and 3. $210; 4. $195; 5 thru 7. $175; 8 thru 23. $150; 24 thru 42. $125; 43 thru 53. $100; 54 thru 65. $85; 66 thru 70. $75; 71 thru 74. $50.

Boyle, Jack
1. $85.

Bradbury, Ray
1. $475; 2. $275; 3. $150; 4. $100; 5. $75; 6. $175; 7. $160; 8. $75; 9. $150; 10 and 11. $75; 12 thru 15. $100; 16 and 17. $125; 18. $65; 19 thru 24. $75; 25. $100; 26. $75; 27. $60; 28. $105; 29 thru 31. $65; 32 and 33. $55; 34. $40.

Bradford, Richard
1. $25; 2. $20.

Bragg, W.F.
1. $40; 2 thru 18. $25; 19 thru 21. $20.

Brahms, Caryl
1. $65; 2 and 3. $50; 4 thru 14. $45; 15 thru 18. $35; 19 thru 26. $25; 27 thru 32. $20.

Bramah, Ernest
1. $250; 2 and 3. $175; 4. $100; 5. $175; 6. $550; 7. $200; 8. $550; 9. $400; 10. $350; 11. $175; 12. $75; 13 and 14. $65; 15. $350; 16. $150; 17. $135; 18. $350.

Brand, Christianna
1 and 2. $65; 3. $50; 4 thru 8. $40; 9 thru 15. $35; 16 thru 20. $25; 21 thru 26. $20.

Brandon, John G.
1. $75; 2 thru 7. $50; 8 thru 72. $40; 73. $30; 74 thru 108. $40; 109 and 110. $35; 111 thru 120. $25.

Branson, H.C.
1. $40; 2 thru 5. $30; 6 and 7. $25; 8. $20; 9. $15.

Braun, Lillian Jackson
1. $35; 2 and 3. $25.

Braun, Matt
1 and 2. $45; 3 thru 14. $35; 15 and 16. $25; 17 thru 20. $20; 21. $15.

Brean, Herbert
1. $25; 2 thru 9. $20; 10 thru 15. $15.

Brent, Madeleine
1. $35; 2 thru 6. $25; 7. $20.

Brett, Simon
1. $25; 2 thru 7. $20.

Brewer, Gil
1 thru 3. $35; 4 thru 19. $25; 20 thru 33. $20.

Bridge, Ann
1. $65; 2 thru 8. $50; 9 thru 17. $35; 18 thru 25. $25; 26 thru 28. $20.

Bridges, Victor
1. $65; 2 thru 7. $40; 8 thru 15. $35; 16 thru 31. $25; 32 thru 44. $20.

Brittain, William
1. $20; 2. $15.

Brock, Lynn
1. $65; 2 thru 20. $50; 21 thru 24. $35.

Bromfield, Louis
1. $125; 2 thru 6. $90; 7 thru 20. $75; 21 thru 23. $60; 24. $50.

Brown, Dee
1. $125; 2 thru 9. $75; 10 thru 16. $60; 17 thru 25. $50; 26 and 27. $35.

Brown, Fredric
1. $125.

Brown, J.P.S.
1. $35; 2 thru 4. $25.

Burchardt, Bill
1. $35; 2 and 3. $25; 4 thru 7. $20; 8 thru 10. $15.

Burford, Lolah
1. $35; 2 thru 4. $25; 5. $20; 6. $15.

Burgess, Anthony
1. $125; 2. $650; 3. $50; 4. $75.

Burgess, Gelett
1. $160; 2. $150; 3. $500; 4. $150.

Burke, John
1. $125; 2 thru 20. $75; 21 thru 63. $65; 64 thru 91. $50.

Burnett, Frances Hodgson
1. $250; 2. $450; 3. $115; 4 and 5. $225.

Burnett, W.R.
1. $150; 2 and 3. $85; 4 thru 37. $65.

Burns, Walter Noble
1. $125; 2 thru 4. $100; 5 and 6. $65.

Burroughs, Edgar Rice
1. $5,000; 2. $800; 3. $750; 4. $800; 5. $2,400; 6. $675; 7. $1,000; 8. $500; 9. $850; 10. $500; 11 and 12. $750; 13 and 14. $500; 15. $425; 16. $650; 17. $750; 18 and 19. $350; 20. $600; 21. $900; 22. $750; 23. $800; 24 and 25. $525; 26. $300; 27 thru 29. $350; 30. $750; 31. $210; 32. $195; 33 and 34. $300; 35. $340; 36 and 37. $225; 38. $150; 39 thru 44. $250; 45. $200; 46. $250; 47. $225; 48. $255; 49. $125; 50. $340; 51 and 52. $300; 53. $175; 54. $150; 55. $225; 56. $100; 57 and 58. $225; 59. $525; 60. $135; 61. $225; 62 thru 64. $175; 65 and 66. $125; 67 thru 73. $70; 74. $75; 75. $70.

Burt, Katharine
1. $65; 2 thru 9. $50; 10 thru 21. $35; 22 thru 25. $25; 26 thru 30. $20.

Busch, Niven
1. $50; 2 thru 4. $35; 5 thru 11. $25; 12 and 13. $20.

Bush, Christopher
1. $85; 2 thru 50. $65; 51 thru 60. $50; 61 thru 84. $40; 85 thru 95. $30.

Butler, Gwendoline
1. $45; 2 thru 5. $35; 6 thru 22. $30; 23 thru 38. $25; 39. $20.

Butler, Octavia E.
1. $35; 2 thru 4. $25; 5. $20.

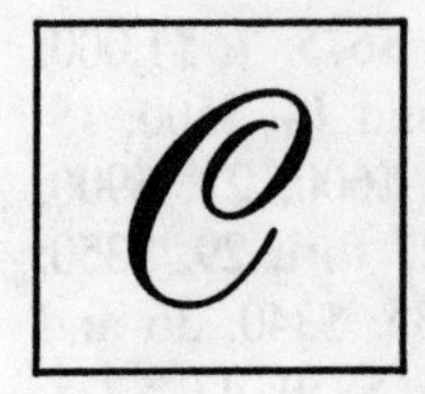

Cadell, Elizabeth
1. $35; 2 thru 6. $25; 7 thru 56. $20; 57 thru 59. $15.

Caine, Hall
1. $175; 2 thru 20. $125; 21 thru 30. $90; 31 and 32. $50; 33. $35.

Caird, Janet
1. $45; 2 thru 6. $30; 7 thru 9. $25; 10. $20.

Caldwell, Taylor
1. $65; 2 thru 9. $50; 10 thru 13. $35; 14 thru 22. $30; 23 thru 33. $25; 34 thru 43. $20; 44. $15.

Cameron, Lou
1. $35; 2 thru 16. $25; 17 thru 45. $20; 46 thru 49. $15.

Capps, Benjamin
1. $35; 2 thru 6. $25; 7 thru 11. $20.

Carter, Felicity
1. $50; 2 thru 5. $40; 6 thru 8. $35; 9. $30; 10 thru 14. $25; 15 and 16. $20.

Carter, Forrest
1. $75; 2. $60; 3 thru 5. $50; 6. $35; 7. $30.

Case, David
1 and 2. $35; 3 thru 6. $25; 7 and 8. $20; 9. $35; 10 and 11. $20; 12. $25.

Case, Robert Ormond
1. $50; 2 thru 16. $35; 17 and 18. $30; 19. $25; 20 and 21. $20.

Cather, Willa
1. $1,200; 2. $450; 3. $375; 4. $425; 5. $300; 6. $375; 7. $600; 8. $125; 9. $115; 10. $125; 11 and 12. $100; 13. $50; 14 and 15. $100; 16. $1,500; 17. $75; 18 thru 25. $60; 26. $45; 27. $35; 28. $50; 29. $35.

Charbonneau, Louis
1. $45; 2 thru 21. $35; 22 thru 34. $25; 35 and 36. $20.

Charles, Theresa
1. $125; 2. $100; 3 thru 53. $90; 54 thru 94. $75; 95 thru 118. $60; 119 thru 168. $50; 169 thru 216. $40; 217 thru 246. $30; 247 thru 252. $20.

Chase, Borden
1. $45; 2. $35; 3 thru 7. $25.

Chisholm, A.M.
1. $50; 2 thru 13. $35.

Christie, Agatha
1. $2,250; 2 and 3. $500; 4 thru 21. $325; 22 thru 31. $275; 32. $750; 33 thru 43. $275; 44. $675; 45 thru 48. $275; 49. $750; 50 thru 58. $275; 59. $750; 60 thru 88. $275; 89 thru 122. $225; 123 thru 144. $175; 145 thru 155. $125; 156 and 157. $75; 158. $50.

Clark, Walter Van Tilburg
1. $400; 2. $125; 3. $75; 4. $45; 5 thru 7. $35.

Cleve, Brian
1 and 2. $65; 3 thru 5. $50; 6 thru 15. $40; 16. $100; 17. $40; 18 thru 28. $35; 29 thru 31. $60.

Coburn, Walt
1. $75; 2 thru 9. $60; 10 thru 29. $35; 30 thru 39. $25.

Cockrell, Marian
1. $40; 2 thru 5. $30; 6. $25; 7 thru 9. $20.

Cody, Stetson
1. $50; 2 thru 14. $40; 15 thru 23. $30; 24. $25.

Coffman, Virginia
1. $50; 2 thru 31. $40; 32 thru 71. $30; 72 thru 75. $20.

Coldsmith, Don
1. —; 2. $25; 3 and 4. $15.

Comfort, Will
1. —; 2. $85; 3 thru 17. $50; 18 thru 25. $40; 26 thru 29. $35.

Conner, Ralph
1 thru 3. $85; 4 thru 19. $65; 20 thru 25. $50; 26 thru 30. $40; 31 thru 39. $30.

Constiner, Merle
1. $40; 2 and 3. $30; 4 thru 14. $25; 15 thru 17. $20.

Cook, Will
1. $45; 2 thru 26. $35; 27 thru 56. $25; 57 and 58. $20.

Cook, William Wallace
1. $65; 2 thru 4. $50; 5 thru 41. $35.

Cookson, Catherine
1. $50; 2 thru 11. $40; 12 thru 35. $30; 36 thru 59. $25; 60 thru 66. $20.

Coolidge, Dane
1. $165; 2 thru 8. $150; 9 thru 17. $125; 18 thru 22. $100; 23. $150; 24 thru 47. $100.

Cooper, Courtney Ryley
1. $85; 2 thru 4. $65; 5 thru 23. $50; 24 thru 35. $40.

Cord, Barry
1. $35; 2 thru 24. $25; 25 thru 39. $20; 40 thru 49. $15.

Corelli, Marie
1 and 2. $225; 3 thru 15. $175; 16. $125; 17 and 18. $100; 19 thru 34. $85; 35 thru 43. $75; 44 thru 49. $65; 50. $35.

Corle, Edwin
1. $85; 2. $65; 3. $55; 4 thru 7. $50; 8 thru 13. $40; 14 and 15. $35; 16. $85; 17. $30.

Cort, Van
1 and 2. $35; 3 and 4. $25.

Costain, Thomas B.
1. $125; 2 thru 4. $85; 5 thru 7. $65; 8 thru 17. $50; 18. $40; 19 thru 22. $35.

Coulson, Juanita
1. $35; 2. $25; 3 thru 11. $20; 12 thru 14. $15.

Coulson, John H.A.
1. $65; 2 thru 4. $50; 5 thru 8. $35; 9 thru 15. $25.

Courtney, Caroline
1 thru 5. $25; 6 thru 12. $20.

Cowen, Frances
1. $65; 2 thru 10. $50; 11 thru 17. $40; 18 thru 31. $35; 32 thru 58. $30; 59 thru 61. $25.

Cox, A.B.
1. $125; 2 thru 13. $100; 14 thru 32. $85; 33. $65.

Cox, William R.
1. $40; 2 thru 7. $30; 8 thru 34. $25; 35 thru 66. $20.

Craig, Mary Francis
1. $45; 2 thru 10. $35; 11 thru 26. $25; 27 thru 30. $20.

Crowe, Cecily
1. $35; 2 and 3. $25; 4 thru 6. $20.

Cullum, Ridgewell
1 and 2. $85; 3 thru 9. $65; 10 thru 22. $50; 23 thru 33. $40; 34 thru 39. $35; 40. $25.

Culp, John H.
1. $25; 2 thru 8. $20.

Cunningham, Chet
1. $35; 2 thru 21. $25; 22 thru 28. $20.

Cunningham, Eugene
1. $275; 2 thru 6. $200; 7 thru 22. $175; 23 and 24. $150; 25 and 26. $90.

Curry, Peggy Simson
1. $35; 2. $25; 3. $20; 4 and 5. $15.

Curwood, James Oliver
1. $175; 2 thru 4. $140; 5 thru 26. $125; 27 thru 39. $100; 40 thru 42. $85; 43. $65; 44. $50.

Cushman, Dan
1. $50; 2 thru 18. $40; 19 thru 30. $30; 31 thru 33. $20.

Dailey, Janet
1 and 2. $35; 3 thru 44. $30; 45 thru 70. $20.

Daniels, Dorothy
1. $50; 2 thru 55. $40; 56 thru 147. $30; 148 thru 157. $20.

Darcy, Clare
1. $25; 2 thru 12. $20; 13 and 14. $15.

Davenport, Marcia
1. $35; 2 and 3. $25; 4 thru 9. $20.

Davis, Dorothy Salisbury
1. $65; 2 thru 4. $50; 5 thru 8. $40; 9 thru 14. $30; 15 thru 17. $25; 18. $20.

Davis, H.L.
1. $50; 2. $40; 3. $35; 4. $30; 5 thru 8. $25.

Dawson, Peter
1 thru 6. $35; 7 thru 12. $25; 13 thru 29. $20.

Day, Robert S.
1. $20.

Dean, Dudley
1. $35; 2 thru 20. $25; 21 thru 29. $20.

Decker, William
1. $25; 2. $20.

Deeping, Warwick
1. $85; 2 thru 10. $65; 11 thru 27. $50; 28 thru 40. $40; 41 thru 67. $35; 68 thru 76. $30; 77 thru 81. $25; 82 thru 88. $20.

Delafield, E.M.
1. $50; 2 thru 4. $40; 5 thru 19. $35; 20 thru 45. $30.

Dell, Ethel M.
1. $65; 2 thru 13. $50; 14 thru 31. $40; 32 thru 44. $30.

Delmar, Vina
1. $50; 2 thru 12. $40; 13 thru 19. $30; 20 thru 24. $25; 25 and 26. $20.

Denver, Lee
1. $35; 2 thru 4. $30; 5 thru 10. $25; 11 thru 19. $20.

De Rosso, H.A.
1 and 2. $35; 3. $30; 4. $25; 5 and 6. $20.

De Voto, Bernard
1. $75; 2 thru 16. $50; 17. $225; 18 thru 22. $40; 23. $35.

DeWeese-Wehen, Joy
1. $25; 2 thru 7. $20.

Dewlen, Al
1. $35; 2 thru 5. $25; 6 and 7. $20; 8. $15.

Doctorow, E.L.
1. $125; 2. $85; 3. $75; 4. $60; 5. $35; 6. $30; 7. $25.

Dowler, James R.
1. $25; 2 thru 4. $15.

Drago, Harry Sinclair
1. $225; 2. $175; 3 thru 17. $165; 18 thru 69. $150; 70 thru 82. $100; 83 thru 109. $85; 110 thru 126. $65; 127 thru 130. $50.

Dresser, Davis
1 and 2. $85; 3 thru 19. $75; 20 thru 50. $65; 51 thru 76. $50; 77 thru 102. $40; 103 thru 112. $30.

Durham, Marilyn
1. $25; 2 and 3. $20.

Durst, Paul
1. $45; 2 thru 21. $35; 22 thru 25. $25; 26 thru 28. $20.

Dunnett, Dorothy
1. $35; 2 thru 6. $25; 7 thru 15. $20; 16. $15.

Dymoke, Juliet
1. $35; 2 thru 7. $25; 8 thru 18. $20; 19 thru 21. $15.

Eastlake, William
1. $190; 2. $75; 3 thru 5. $65; 6. $35; 7. $50; 8. $25.

Easton, Robert
1. $50; 2 thru 6. $35; 7. $25; 8 and 9. $20.

Eberhart, Mignon G.
1. $85; 2 thru 20. $75; 21 thru 37. $60; 38 thru 47. $50; 48 thru 58. $40; 59 thru 66. $30; 67 thru 69. $25.

Eden, Dorothy
1. $65; 2 thru 6. $50; 7 thru 17. $40; 18 thru 39. $30; 40 thru 50. $25; 51 and 52. $20.

Edson, J.T.
1. $50; 2 thru 62. $40; 63 thru 89. $30; 90 thru 105. $25; 106 thru 114. $20.

Ehrlich, Jack
1. $50; 2 thru 8. $35; 9 thru 13. $25.

Eliot, Anne
1. $45; 2 thru 5. $35; 6. $25; 7. $60; 8 thru 19. $25; 20 thru 28. $20.

Elizabeth
1. $125; 2 thru 10. $85; 11 thru 13. $75; 14 thru 19. $65; 20. $50; 21. $40; 22. $35; 23 and 24. $25.

Ellerbeck, Rosemary
1. $65; 2 and 3. $35; 4 thru 8. $25; 9 thru 14. $20.

Elmore, Ernest
1. $85; 2 thru 10. $65; 11 thru 16. $50; 17 thru 24. $40; 25 thru 37. $35.

Elston, Allen Vaughan
1. $65; 2 thru 8. $45; 9 thru 37. $35; 38 thru 40. $25.

Erdman, Loula Grace
1 thru 4. $35; 5 thru 12. $30; 13 thru 18. $25; 19 and 20. $20.

Ertz, Susan
1. $65; 2 thru 7. $50; 8 thru 17. $40; 18 and 19. $30; 20 thru 23. $25; 24 thru 27. $20.

Estleman, Loren D.
1. $35; 2 thru 5. $25; 6 thru 12. $20.

Estridge, Robin
1. $45; 2 thru 13. $35; 14 thru 21. $25; 22 thru 25. $20.

Evans, Max
1. $35; 2 thru 7. $30; 8. $25; 9 and 10. $20.

Evarts, Sr., Hal G.
1. $65; 2 thru 12. $50; 13 thru 18. $40; 19. $35.

Evarts, Jr., Hal G.
1. $50; 2 thru 12. $40; 13 thru 23. $30; 24 thru 28. $25.

Farnol, Jeffery
1. $85; 2 thru 13. $70; 14 thru 25. $65; 26 thru 47. $60; 48 thru 51. $50; 52 thru 55. $40.

Faust, Frederick
1. $350; 2 thru 65. $275; 66 thru 125. $250; 126 thru 164. $225; 165 thru 188. $200; 189 thru 213. $175; 214. $65; 215. $50.

Felton, Ronald
1. $35; 2 thru 10. $30; 11 thru 15. $25; 16 thru 20. $20.

Field, Rachel
1. $75; 2 thru 14. $65; 15 thru 33. $50; 34 thru 39. $35; 40. $25; 41. $20.

Finley, Glenna
1. $35; 2 thru 4. $30; 5 thru 29. $25; 30 thru 34. $20.

Franken, Rose
1. $45; 2 thru 16. $35; 17 thru 20. $25; 21 thru 28. $20.

Freeman, Cynthia
1. $35; 2 thru 4. $25; 5 and 6. $20.

Gallagher, Patricia
1. $35; 2. $30; 3 and 4. $25; 5 thru 10. $20; 11. $15.

Garvice, Charles
1. $125; 2 thru 12. $100; 13 thru 77. $85; 78 thru 117. $75; 118 thru 176. $65; 177. $35.

Gaskin, Catherine
1. $50; 2. $40; 3 thru 7. $30; 8 thru 17. $25; 18 and 19. $20.

Gavin, Catherine
1. $45; 2 thru 7. $35; 8 thru 18. $25; 19. $20.

Gellis, Roberta
1. $25; 2 thru 12. $20; 13 thru 16. $15.

Gibbs, Henry
1. $50; 2 thru 19. $40; 20 thru 53. $35; 54 thru 71. $30; 72 thru 76. $25.

Gibbs, Mary Ann
1. $50; 2 thru 8. $45; 9 thru 24. $40; 25 thru 41. $35; 42 thru 61. $30; 62 thru 65. $25.

Gilbert, Anna
1. $35; 2 thru 5. $25; 6 and 7. $20.

Giles, Janice Holt
1. $45; 2 thru 10. $35; 11 thru 20. $30; 21 thru 24. $25.

Glasscock, Anne
1. $25; 2 thru 4. $20.

Gluyas, Constance
1. $25; 2 thru 11. $20; 12 thru 14. $15.

Glyn, Elinor
1. $125; 2 thru 8. $100; 9 thru 19. $85; 20 thru 31. $75; 32 thru 39. $65; 40. $20.

Godden, Rumer
1. $60; 2 thru 6. $45; 7 thru 14. $40; 15 thru 24. $35; 25 thru 38. $30; 39 thru 48. $25; 49 thru 51. $20.

Gordon, Ethel Edison
1. $25; 2 thru 7. $20; 8. $15.

Goudge, Elizabeth
1. $75; 2 thru 7. $65; 8 thru 17. $50; 18 thru 25. $40; 26 thru 34. $30; 35 thru 41. $25; 42 thru 45. $20.

Greig, Maysie
1. $65; 2 thru 4. $50; 5 thru 113. $45; 114 thru 135. $40; 136 thru 182. $35; 183 thru 222. $30; 223 thru 228. $25.

Grimstead, Hettie
1. $50; 2 thru 24. $35; 25 thru 58. $30; 59 thru 76. $25.

Grundy, Mabel Barnes
1. $45; 2 thru 12. $35; 13 thru 18. $30; 19 thru 23. $25; 24. $20.

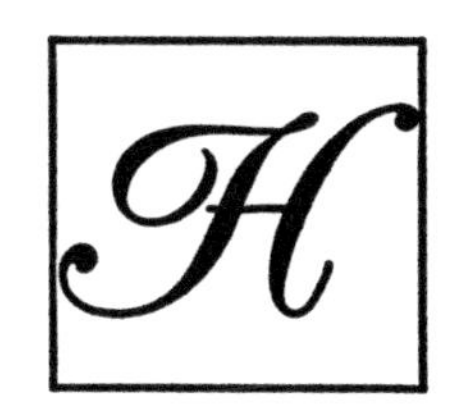

Haas, Ben
1. $35; 2 thru 13. $30; 14 thru 26. $25.

Haggard, H. Rider
1. $525; 2. $1,650; 3 thru 5. $600; 6. $375; 7 thru 45. $150; 46 thru 73. $125; 74. $35; 75. $25.

Haggard, William
1 and 2. $35; 3 thru 14. $25; 15 thru 26. $20.

Haines, Pamela
1. $25; 2 and 3. $20; 4. $15.

Hall, Oakley
1. $35; 2 thru 7. $30; 8 thru 11. $25; 12 thru 18. $20; 19. $15.

Halleran, E.E.
1. $50; 2 thru 9. $40; 10 thru 22. $35; 23 thru 37. $25; 38. $20.

Hamilton, Donald
1. $35; 2 thru 10. $30; 11 thru 24. $25; 25 thru 32. $20.

Hammett, Dashiell
1. $3,000; 2. $1,500; 3. $3,700; 4 and 5. $1,500; 6. $675; 7. $150; 8 thru 21. $300; 22. $225; 23. $175; 24. $125; 25. $85.

Hampson, Anne
1 thru 4. $30; 5 thru 82. $25; 83 thru 94. $20.

Hanshew, Thomas W.
1. $125; 2 thru 4. $100; 5 thru 10. $85; 11 thru 20. $75.

Harbage, Alfred B.
1. $50; 2 and 3. $40; 4 thru 10. $35; 11 and 12. $30; 13 and 14. $25; 15. $20.

Hardwick, Mollie
1. $45; 2 thru 11. $35; 12 thru 37. $25; 38 thru 42. $20.

Hardy, W.G.
1. $35; 2 and 3. $25; 4 thru 13. $20.

Harling, Robert
1. $35; 2 thru 5. $25; 6 thru 12. $20; 13. $35; 14. $20.

Harrington, Joseph
1. $25; 2 thru 5. $20.

Harris, Herbert
1. $25; 2 thru 4. $20.

Harris, Marilyn
1. $25; 2 thru 12. $20.

Harris, Rosemary
1. $65; 2. $50; 3 thru 7. $40; 8 thru 20. $35; 21 thru 23. $25.

Harrison, Elizabeth
1. $35; 2 thru 13. $25.

Harrison, Michael
1. $60; 2 thru 13. $45; 14 thru 19. $40; 20 thru 35. $35; 36 thru 45. $30; 46 thru 56. $25.

Harvey, John B.
1. $45; 2. $35; 3 thru 40. $25; 41 thru 61. $20.

Hastings, Phyllis
1. $45; 2 thru 14. $35; 15 and 16. $30; 17. $65; 18 thru 28. $30; 29 thru 41. $25; 42 thru 45. $20.

Haycox, Ernest
1. $75; 2 thru 24. $45; 25 thru 51. $40; 52 thru 59. $35; 60 thru 63. $25.

Hayes, Joseph
1. $50; 2 thru 15. $40; 16 thru 28. $35; 29 thru 32. $30; 33 thru 37. $25.

Heald, Tim
1. $35; 2 thru 9. $25.

Heaven, Constance
1. $35; 2 thru 6. $30; 7 thru 19. $25; 20 thru 23. $20.

Heckelmann, Charles N.
1 thru 3. $50; 4 thru 11. $40; 12 thru 21. $35; 22 thru 25. $25; 26 and 27. $20.

Hendryx, James B.
1. $75; 2 thru 5. $55; 6 thru 24. $50; 25 thru 47. $45; 48 thru 54. $40; 55 thru 62. $35; 63. $25.

Henry, O.
1. $900; 2 thru 4. $450; 5 thru 7. $375; 8 thru 10. $225; 11 thru 13. $175; 14 thru 16. $150; 17 thru 20. $125; 21 and 22. $100; 23. $75; 24 thru 26. $60; 27 and 28. $50.

Herron, Shaun
1. $25; 2 thru 9. $20.

Heuman, William
1 and 2. $45; 3 thru 37. $35; 38 thru 68. $30; 69 thru 73. $25.

Heyer, Georgette
1. $65; 2 thru 10. $50; 11 thru 33. $45; 34 thru 36. $40; 37 thru 48. $35; 49 thru 55. $25; 56 thru 58. $20.

Hichens, Robert
1. $100; 2 thru 11. $60; 12 thru 24. $55; 25 thru 32. $50; 33 thru 41. $45; 42 thru 60. $40; 61 thru 64. $35; 65 thru 68. $25.

Higgins, George V.
1. $50; 2 thru 8. $35; 9. $25.

Hildick, Wallace
1 and 2. $50; 3 thru 36. $35; 37 thru 72. $30.

Hill, Grace Livingston
1. $75; 2 thru 14. $60; 15 thru 29. $55; 30 thru 49. $50; 50 thru 102. $45; 103 thru 108. $35; 109. $20.

Hill, Pamela
1. $40; 2 thru 4. $35; 5 thru 7. $30; 8 thru 18. $25; 19 thru 22. $20.

Hillerman, Tony
1 and 2. $35; 3 thru 8. $25.

Hilton, James
1. $175; 2 thru 7. $160; 8 thru 21. $150; 22 thru 24. $75; 25 thru 28. $50.

Himes, Chester
1. $225; 2. $175; 3 thru 8. $150; 9 thru 16. $135; 17 and 18. $125; 19. $100; 20. $85; 21. $65.

Hintze, Naomi A.
1. $35; 2. $30; 3 thru 8. $25.

Hobart, Donald Bayne
1. $50; 2 thru 4. $35; 5 and 6. $30; 7 thru 12. $25; 13 thru 25. $20.

Hoch, Edward D.
1. $50; 2 thru 9. $35.

Hocking, Anne
1. $50; 2 thru 34. $40; 35 thru 39. $35; 40 thru 56. $30; 57 thru 60. $25.

Hodge, Jane Aiken
1. $40; 2 thru 6. $35; 7 thru 17. $30; 18 and 19. $25.

Hodgson, William Hope
1. $500; 2 thru 4. $375; 5 thru 12. $325; 13 and 14. $275; 15. $150; 16 and 17. $75.

Hoffman, Lee
1 and 2. $35; 3 thru 12. $30; 13 thru 22. $25.

Hogan, Ray
1. $35; 2 thru 10. $35; 11 thru 62. $30; 63 thru 120. $25; 121 thru 133. $20.

Holding, Elisabeth Sanxay
1. $45; 2 thru 7. $30; 8 thru 20. $25; 21 thru 29. $20.

Holding, James
1. $35; 2 thru 12. $25; 13 and 14. $20.

Holland, Isabelle
1. $35; 2 thru 19. $25; 20 thru 23. $20.

Holland, Sheila
1. $35; 2 thru 51. $25; 52 thru 76. $20.

Holman, C. Hugh
1. $45; 2 thru 5. $35; 6. $30; 7 thru 15. $20.

Holt, Victoria
1 and 2. $50; 3 thru 12. $40; 13 thru 64. $35; 65. $50; 66 thru 103. $30; 104 thru 143. $25; 144 thru 157. $20.

Hope, Anthony
1. $500; 2 thru 6. $425; 7. $375; 8 thru 21. $300; 22 thru 34. $250; 35 thru 41. $225; 42. $175; 43. $85; 44 and 45. $125; 46 and 47. $100.

Hopson, William L.
1. $45; 2 thru 20. $35; 21 thru 47. $30; 48 thru 51. $25; 52 and 53. $20.

Horgan, Paul
1. $275; 2 thru 10. $225; 11 and 12. $175; 13 and 14. $150; 15 thru 17. $125; 18. $375; 19 thru 23. $100; 24 thru 37. $75; 38 thru 44. $65; 45. $50.

Horler, Sydney
1. $50; 2 thru 30. $35; 31 thru 121. $30; 122 thru 176. $25.

Horner, Lance
1. $35; 2 thru 11. $25; 12 thru 14. $20.

Hornung, E.W.
1. $450; 2 thru 12. $350; 13 thru 21. $325; 22 thru 25. $275; 26 thru 33. $225; 34. $175; 35. $150; 36. $35.

Hosken, Clifford
1. $45; 2 thru 6. $35; 7 thru 22. $25; 23. $20.

Hough, Emerson
1. $500; 2. $350; 3. $325; 4 and 5. $275; 6. $150; 7. $275; 8. $250; 9. $225; 10. $125; 11 thru 14. $175; 15. $100; 16 thru 25. $150; 26. $75; 27 thru 34. $125; 35. $50.

Hough, S.B.
1. $45; 2 thru 17. $35; 18 thru 29. $30; 30. $25.

Household, Geoffrey
1. $325; 2 thru 6. $225; 7 thru 16. $175; 17 thru 24. $125; 25 thru 32. $85; 33. $40.

Houston, Tex
1 thru 3. $25.

Howard, Mary
1. $50; 2 thru 15. $40; 16 thru 23. $35; 24 thru 36. $30; 37 thru 48. $25; 49 thru 62. $20.

Howard, Robert E.
1. $2,250; 2. $625; 3. $300; 4 thru 8. $225; 9. $150; 10. $375; 11. $340; 12 thru 16. $375; 17 thru 24. $275; 25 thru 42. $225; 43. $125; 44 thru 49. $150.

Howatch, Susan
1 thru 5. $25; 6 thru 10. $20.

Hoy, Elizabeth
1. $50; 2 thru 23. $40; 24 thru 34. $35; 35 thru 50. $30; 51 thru 62. $25; 63 thru 70. $20; 71. $15.

Huffaker, Clair
1 and 2. $35; 3 thru 7. $30; 8 thru 10. $25; 11 thru 16. $20.

Hufford, Susan
1 thru 8. $25; 9. $20.

Hughes, Dorothy B.
1. $50; 2. $40; 3 thru 14. $30; 15 thru 18. $25; 19 and 20. $20.

Hull, E.M.
1. $175; 2 thru 6. $125; 7. $75; 8. $65.

Hull, Richard
1. $40; 2 thru 9. $35; 10 thru 12. $30; 13 thru 15. $25.

Hume, Fergus
1 and 2. $350; 3 thru 5. $325; 6 thru 48. $300; 49 thru 97. $275; 98 thru 129. $250; 130 thru 139. $225; 140. $175; 141. $150.

Humphrey, William
1. $150; 2. $100; 3 thru 5. $85; 6 thru 10. $65.

Hunter, Elizabeth
1 and 2. $45; 3 thru 25. $30; 26 thru 58. $25; 59 thru 61. $20.

Hunter, Evan
1. $175; 2 thru 6. $150; 7. $225; 8 thru 34. $150; 35 thru 61. $125; 62 thru 85. $85; 86. $65.

Hurst, Fannie
1. $65; 2 thru 4. $45; 5 thru 13. $40; 14 thru 23. $35; 24. $30; 25 thru 28. $25; 29 thru 31. $20.

Hutten, Baroness von
1. $45; 2 thru 12. $35; 13 thru 21. $30; 22 thru 28. $25; 29 thru 41. $20.

Huxley, Elspeth
1. $65; 2 thru 6. $40; 7 thru 16. $35; 17 thru 26. $30; 27 thru 31. $25; 32. $20.

Inglis, Susan
1. $45; 2 thru 11. $35; 12 thru 14. $30; 15 thru 22. $25; 23. $20.

Irwin, Margaret
1. $65; 2 and 3. $45; 4 thru 10. $40; 11 thru 23. $35; 24. $30; 25 and 26. $25; 27. $20.

Jackson, Shirley
1. $225; 2. $190; 3. $175; 4. $150; 5. $135; 6 thru 11. $125; 12. $100; 13. $85; 14 thru 17. $75.

Jacob, Naomi
1. $65; 2 thru 6. $40; 7 thru 41. $35; 42 thru 68. $30; 69 thru 78. $25.

Jakes, John
1. $85; 2 thru 8. $50; 9 thru 28. $45; 29 thru 64. $40; 65 thru 68. $35; 69. $25.

James, P.D.
1. $50; 2 and 3. $35; 4 thru 8. $25.

James, Will
1. $275; 2 and 3. $225; 4 and 5. $175; 6 thru 10. $150; 11 thru 23. $75; 24. $35.

Jarrett, Cora
1. $35; 2 thru 7. $25; 8. $20.

Jay, G.M.
1. $75; 2 thru 9. $50; 10 thru 12. $40; 13 thru 16. $35.

Jeffries, Roderic
1. $75; 2 thru 16. $55; 17 thru 59. $50; 60 thru 90. $45; 91. $35.

Jenkins, W.F.
1 and 2. $75; 3 thru 17. $55; 18 thru 46. $50; 47 thru 72. $45; 73. $35.

Jenks, George C.
1. $225; 2 and 3. $175; 4 thru 6. $85.

Jepson, Selwyn
1 and 2. $85; 3 thru 11. $60; 12 thru 19. $55; 20. $50; 21 thru 31. $45; 32 thru 36. $40; 37. $35.

Jessup, Richard
1. $45; 2 thru 12. $35; 13 thru 19. $30; 20 thru 22. $25; 23. $20.

Johnson, Barbara Ferry
1 thru 4. $20; 5. $15.

Johnson, Dorothy M.
1. $65; 2. $40; 3 and 4. $35; 5 thru 11. $30; 12 thru 19. $25; 20. $20.

Johnson, E. Richard
1. $35; 2 thru 4. $25; 5 thru 9. $20.

Johnston, Mary
1. $135; 2 thru 8. $100; 9 thru 19. $85; 20 thru 25. $65; 26 thru 28. $50.

Johnston, Norma
1. $40; 2 thru 4. $30; 5 thru 19. $25; 20 and 21. $20.

Johnston, Velda
1. $40; 2 thru 4. $30; 5 thru 20. $25; 21 thru 24. $20.

Jones, Douglas C.
1. $50; 2 thru 5. $35; 6 thru 9. $25.

Jones, Nard
1. $65; 2 thru 9. $40; 10 thru 12. $35; 13 thru 15. $30; 16 and 17. $25.

Joscelyn, Archie
1. $75; 2 thru 49. $45; 50 thru 147. $40; 148 thru 195. $35; 196 thru 220. $30.

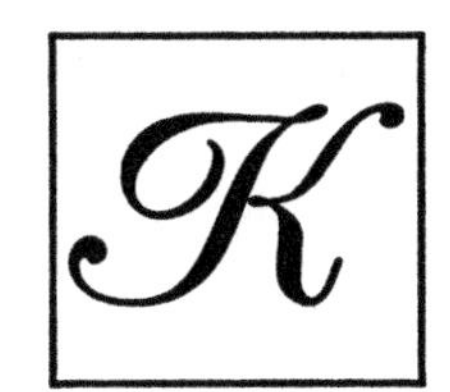

Kane, Frank
1. $40; 2 and 3. $30; 4 thru 21. $25; 22 thru 43. $20.

Kane, Henry
1. $45; 2 thru 4. $35; 5 thru 32. $30; 33 thru 65. $25; 66 thru 82. $20.

Kantor, MacKinlay
1. $125; 2 thru 11. $100; 12 thru 16. $85; 17 thru 21. $75; 22 thru 24. $65; 25 thru 29. $50; 30. $75; 31 thru 39. $40; 40 thru 47. $35; 48 thru 51. $30.

Keating, H.R.F.
1. $65; 2 thru 11. $45; 12 thru 25. $35.

Keene, Day
1. $50; 2. $40; 3 thru 37. $35; 38 thru 47. $30; 48 and 49. $25.

Kelland, Clarence Budington
1. $75; 2. $100; 3. $165; 4 thru 9. $45; 10 and 11. $40; 12. $75; 13. $65; 14 thru 23. $40; 24 thru 46. $35; 47 thru 65. $30; 66 thru 70. $25.

Kelton, Elmer
1. $50; 2 thru 4. $35; 5 thru 14. $30; 15 thru 23. $25; 24 thru 26. $20.

Kennedy, Margaret
1. $90; 2 and 3. $75; 4 thru 7. $65; 8 thru 12. $50; 13 and 14. $40; 15 thru 21. $35; 22 thru 25. $30.

Kennedy, Milward
1. $90; 2 thru 4. $65; 5 thru 20. $55; 21. $45; 22 and 23. $35.

Kenrick, Tony
1. $45; 2 thru 7. $30; 8 and 9. $25; 10. $20.

Kenyon, Michael
1. $40; 2 thru 5. $30; 6 thru 15. $25.

Kersh, Gerald
1. $90; 2 thru 12. $65; 13 thru 22. $55; 23 thru 31. $45; 32 thru 41. $35.

Kesey, Ken
1. $450; 2. $350; 3. $175; 4. $35.

Ketchum, Philip L.
1. $60; 2 and 3. $45; 4 and 5. $40; 6 thru 27. $35; 28 thru 48. $30; 49 thru 52. $25.

Kevern, Barbara
1 thru 4. $25.

Keyes, Frances Parkinson
1. $75; 2 and 3. $50; 4 thru 22. $45; 23 thru 40. $40; 41 thru 50. $35; 51. $25.

Kidd, Flora
1 thru 3. $35; 4 thru 6. $30; 7 thru 36. $25; 37 thru 42. $20.

Kimbrough, Katheryn
1 and 2. $45; 3 thru 48. $35; 49 thru 52. $25.

King, C. Daly
1. $60; 2 thru 7. $45; 8. $35.

King, General Charles
1. $550; 2 thru 11. $85; 12 thru 36. $75; 37 thru 56. $65; 57. $50.

King, Rufus
1. $60; 2 thru 7. $45; 8 thru 25. $40; 26 thru 31. $35; 32 and 33. $30; 34 thru 36. $25.

Kirk, Russell
1. $65; 2 and 3. $45; 4 thru 7. $60; 8. $85.

Knibbs, H.H.
1. $75; 2 thru 10. $55; 11 thru 17. $45; 18 thru 20. $40.

Knight, Alanna
1. $40; 2 thru 14. $30; 15 thru 17. $25.

Knox, Bill
1. $45; 2 and 3. $35; 4 thru 33. $30; 34 thru 59. $25.

Knox, Ronald A.
1. $125; 2 thru 10. $90; 11 thru 22. $80; 23 thru 31. $70; 32. $60; 33 thru 39. $50.

Krause, Herbert
1 and 2. $45; 3. $35; 4. $30; 5. $25.

Kyne, Peter B.
1. $85; 2 thru 11. $65; 12 thru 25. $55; 26 thru 36. $45; 37 and 38. $35.

La Farge, Oliver
1. $65; 2. $60; 3 thru 11. $35; 12 thru 20. $30; 21 thru 23. $25.

L'Amour, Louis
1. $375; 2. $275; 3 thru 7. $225; 8 thru 22. $175; 23 thru 51. $150; 52 thru 79. $125; 80 and 81. $75; 82. $65; 83 and 84. $50.

Lane, Roumelia
1 and 2. $40; 3 thru 6. $30; 7 thru 19. $25; 20. $20.

Langley, John
1. $40; 2 thru 4. $30; 5 thru 16. $25; 17. $20.

Lathen, Emma
1. $95; 2 thru 12. $65; 13 thru 23. $50.

Latimer, Jonathan
1 and 2. $65; 3 thru 8. $50; 9 thru 12. $45; 13. $40.

La Tourrette, Jacqueline
1 thru 6. $25; 7. $20.

Lawrence, Hilda
1. $65; 2 thru 5. $45; 6. $50.

Lea, Tom
1 and 2. $300; 3 thru 5. $1,500; 6. $1,125; 7. $125; 8. $300; 9. $125; 10. $450; 11. $300; 12. $175; 13. $1,200; 14 thru 17. $125; 18. $100.

Leasor, James
1. $60; 2 thru 12. $40; 13 thru 28. $35; 29 thru 37. $30.

le Carre, John
1. $275; 2. $225; 3. $200; 4 and 5. $150; 6 and 7. $125; 8. $100; 9. $75; 10. $60.

Lee, Elsie
1 thru 5. $25; 6 thru 15. $35; 16. $25; 17 thru 20. $35; 21. $25; 22 thru 25. $35; 26 thru 36. $30; 37. $20; 38 thru 41. $25.

Lee, Wayne
1. $45; 2 thru 10. $35; 11 thru 31. $30; 32 thru 45. $25; 46 thru 50. $20.

Lehman, Paul Evan
1 and 2. $65; 3 thru 13. $50; 14 thru 19. $45; 20 thru 66. $40; 67 thru 73. $35.

Lemarchand, Elizabeth
1. $60; 2 and 3. $45; 4 thru 11. $35.

LeMay, Alan
1. $50; 2 and 3. $40; 4 thru 13. $35; 14 and 15. $30; 16 thru 18. $25; 19. $20.

Leonard, Elmore
1. $100; 2 thru 5. $65; 6 thru 10. $55; 11 thru 19. $45; 20 thru 23. $35.

Le Queux, William
1. $375; 2 thru 20. $225; 21 thru 71. $200; 72 thru 150. $175; 151 thru 212. $150; 213 and 214. $125.

Leslie, Doris
1. $60; 2 and 3. $45; 4 thru 13. $40; 14 and 15. $35; 16 thru 21. $30; 22 thru 27. $25; 28 thru 36. $20.

Lesser, Milton
1. $50; 2 thru 20. $40; 21 thru 45. $35; 46 thru 49. $30.

Levin, Ira
1. $125; 2 thru 7. $85; 8 thru 10. $65; 11. $50.

Lewin, Michael Z.
1. $25; 2 thru 8. $35.

Lewis, Alfred Henry
1. $200; 2. $125; 3 thru 14. $100; 15. $75; 16. $100; 17 thru 20. $65; 21 and 22. $35.

Lewis, C. Day
1. $650; 2 and 3. $150; 4 thru 35. $125; 36 thru 62. $100; 63 thru 81. $75; 82 thru 86. $50.

Lewis, Maynah
1. $40; 2 thru 9. $30; 10 and 19. $25; 20 thru 22. $20.

Lewis, Roy
1. $35; 2 thru 16. $20; 17. $25; 18. $20; 19 thru 24. $25; 25. $20; 26 thru 30. $25; 31 and 32. $20; 33 thru 35. $25; 36. $20.

Lewty, Marjorie
1. $45; 2 and 3. $35; 4 thru 7. $30; 8 thru 18. $25; 19 thru 21. $20.

Ley, Alice Chetwynd
1. $40; 2 thru 6. $30; 7 thru 13. $25; 14. $20.

Linebarger, P.M.A.
1. $45; 2 and 3. $25; 4 thru 6. $85; 7. $25; 8. $35; 9 thru 17. $75; 18. $25.

Lindsay, Rachel
1. $45; 2 thru 15. $35; 16 thru 19. $30; 20. $40; 21 thru 27. $30; 28 thru 67. $25; 68 thru 74. $20.

Linington, Elizabeth
1. $75; 2 thru 6. $50; 7 thru 41. $45; 42 thru 66. $40.

Little, Constance and Gwyneth
1 and 2. $75; 3 thru 11. $55; 12 thru 17. $45; 18 thru 23. $35.

Lofts, Norah
1. $65; 2 thru 13. $45; 14 thru 18. $40; 19 thru 28. $35; 29 thru 39. $30; 40 thru 62. $25; 63 thru 65. $20.

London, Jack
1. $1,875; 2. $600; 3. $1,500; 4. $525; 5. $675; 6. $1,500; 7. $225; 8 and 9. $375; 10. $825; 11 thru 13. $375; 14. $675; 15. $125; 16. $675; 17. $750; 18 and 19. $675; 20. $1,500; 21. $375; 22. $525; 23. $1,425; 24. $525; 25. $675; 26. $375; 27. $1,600; 28. $225; 29. $525; 30. $750; 31. $375; 32. $525; 33. $750; 34. $600; 35. $750; 36. $375; 37. $525; 38. $375; 39. $225; 40. $525; 41. $375; 42. $600; 43. $975; 44. $850; 45 thru 49. $375; 50 and 51. $525; 52. $2,000; 53. $525; 54. $375; 55. $1,200; 56. $375; 57. $525; 58. $1,125; 59. $525; 60 and 61. $375; 62. $525; 63. $375; 64. $1,400; 65. $325; 66 thru 70. $125; 71 thru 83. $85.

London, Laura
1 thru 3. $25; 4 and 5. $20.

Loring, Emilie
1. $60; 2 thru 10. $45; 11 thru 28. $40; 29 thru 42. $35; 43 thru 51. $30; 52 thru 54. $25.

Lorrimer, Clair
1. $75; 2 and 3. $50; 4 thru 22. $40; 23 thru 41. $35; 42 thru 51. $30; 52 thru 55. $25.

Lovesey, Peter
1. $35; 2. $100; 3 thru 13. $45; 14. $35.

Low, Dorothy Mackie
1. $40; 2 thru 5. $30; 6 thru 10. $25; 11. $20.

Lowndes, Marie
1 and 2. $85; 3 thru 8. $55; 9 thru 22. $50; 23 thru 36. $45; 37 thru 62. $40; 63 thru 65. $35; 66. $25.

Ludlum, Robert
1. $50; 2 thru 10. $35.

Lyall, Gavin
1. $40; 2 thru 5. $30; 6 thru 8. $25.

Lynn, Margaret
1 thru 5. $25; 6. $20.

Macardle, Dorothy
1 and 2. $50; 3 thru 8. $40; 9. $35; 10 and 11. $25.

MacDonald, John D.
1. $125; 2 thru 33. $75; 34 thru 64. $65; 65 thru 75. $50.

MacDonald, Philip
1. $125; 2 thru 7. $75; 8 thru 35. $65; 36. $45; 37 thru 43. $40; 44. $35.

MacGill, Mrs. Patrick
1. $45; 2 thru 4. $35; 5 thru 19. $25; 20 and 21. $20.

MacInnes, Helen
1 and 2. $125; 3 and 4. $100; 5 thru 7. $75; 8 thru 11. $65; 12 thru 16. $55; 17 thru 20. $45.

Mackinlay, Leila
1. $60; 2 thru 26. $45; 27 thru 54. $40; 55 thru 77. $35; 78 thru 89. $30.

MacLean, Alistair
1. $175; 2 thru 5. $125; 6 thru 15. $100; 16 thru 23. $85; 24 thru 28. $65; 29 thru 33. $50.

MacLeod, Charlotte
1 thru 3. $35; 4 thru 13. $25; 14 thru 20. $20.

MacLeod, Jean S.
1. $60; 2 thru 27. $45; 28 thru 73. $40; 74 thru 101. $35; 102 thru 118. $30; 119. $25.

Maddocks, Margaret
1. $55; 2 and 3. $40; 4 thru 7. $35; 8 thru 14. $30; 15 thru 18. $25.

Mainwaring, Daniel
1. $75; 2 thru 13. $50; 14 thru 17. $40; 18. $35.

Maling, Arthur
1. $35; 2 thru 11. $25.

Manley-Tucker, Audrie
1. $45; 2. $35; 3 thru 17. $30; 18 thru 25. $25; 26 and 27. $20.

Marlowe, Dan J.
1 and 2. $35; 3 thru 16. $25; 17 thru 27. $20.

Marlowe, Derek
1. $45; 2 and 3. $35; 4 thru 9. $25; 10. $20.

Marlowe, Hugh
1. $60; 2 thru 37. $45; 38 thru 56. $35; 57. $25.

Marquand, John
1. $125; 2. $225; 3 thru 6. $175; 7 thru 20. $150; 21 thru 26. $125; 27 thru 34. $100; 35 and 36. $75; 37. $50.

Marsh, Jean
1. $60; 2. $45; 3. $40; 4 thru 11. $35; 12 and 13. $30; 14 thru 17. $25; 18 thru 23. $20.

Marsh, Ngaio
1. $100; 2 thru 14. $75; 15 thru 19. $60; 20 thru 27. $50; 28 thru 36. $45; 37 thru 41. $35.

Marshall, Edison
1. $85; 2 thru 17. $60; 18 thru 33. $55; 34 thru 38. $50; 39 thru 49. $45; 50 thru 54. $40.

Marshall, Rosamond
1. $60; 2. $45; 3 thru 16. $35.

Martin, Rhona
1. $25; 2. $20.

Mason, A.E.W.
1. $425; 2 thru 6. $375; 7 thru 13. $325; 14 thru 20. $300; 21 thru 26. $225; 27 thru 38. $175; 39. $85.

Masur, Harold Q.
1. $45; 2. $35; 3 thru 9. $30; 10 thru 13. $25; 14. $20.

Mather, Anne
1. $35; 2 thru 11. $25; 12 thru 76. $20; 77 thru 85. $15.

Mather, Berkely
1. $60; 2 thru 8. $45; 9 thru 16. $35.

Maugham, Robin
1. $125; 2 thru 7. $75; 8 thru 14. $65; 15 thru 24. $55; 25 thru 36. $45.

Maugham, W. Somerset
1. $1,750; 2 and 3. $400; 4 and 5. $300; 6. $1,200; 7 thru 20. $300; 21. $1,750; 22. $300; 23 thru 39. $275; 40 thru 56. $225; 57. $1,100; 58 thru 62. $225; 63 thru 72. $175; 73 thru 94. $150; 95 and 96. $125; 97 thru 100. $100; 101 and 102. $75.

May, Wynne
1 thru 3. $25; 4 thru 15. $20.

Maybury, Anne
1 thru 4. $45; 5 thru 37. $40; 38 thru 41. $35; 42 thru 57. $30; 58 thru 69. $25; 70 thru 77. $20.

McBain, Laurie
1. $25; 2 thru 4. $20; 5. $15.

McCloy, Helen
1 and 2. $85; 3 thru 9. $65; 10 thru 21. $50; 22 thru 26. $35; 27 thru 34. $25.

McClure, James
1. $35; 2 thru 9. $25.

McCoy, Horace
1. $225; 2. $150; 3. $125; 4. $65; 5 and 6. $45; 7. $25.

McCutchan, Philip
1. $65; 2 thru 5. $45; 6 thru 35. $35; 36 thru 71. $25.

McCutcheon, George Barr
1. $150; 2 thru 16. $125; 17 thru 36. $100; 37 thru 46. $85; 47. $65.

McDonald, Gregory
1. $85; 2 thru 7. $45.

McEvoy, Marjorie
1 and 2. $40; 3 thru 21. $30; 22 thru 33. $25; 34. $20.

McGivern, William P.
1. $50; 2. $40; 3 thru 17. $35; 18 thru 25. $30; 26 thru 30. $25.

McNeile, H.C.
1 and 2. $125; 3 thru 7. $95; 8 thru 21. $85; 22 thru 36. $75.

McShane, Mark
1. $50; 2 thru 12. $40; 13 thru 32. $35.

Meade, L.T.
1. $225; 2 thru 10. $150; 11 thru 38. $140; 39 thru 94. $130; 95 thru 193. $120; 194 thru 240. $110; 241 thru 243. $100.

Meggs, Brown
1. $35; 2. $25; 3. $20.

Meyer, Nicholas
1. $50; 2. $40; 3 and 4. $35.

Meynell, Laurence
1. $100; 2 thru 6. $80; 7 thru 38. $75; 39 thru 46. $70; 47 thru 98. $65; 99 thru 128. $60; 129 thru 157. $50.

Miles, Lady
1 and 2. $35; 3 thru 8. $25; 9 thru 11. $20.

Millar, Margaret
1. $125; 2 thru 5. $100; 6 thru 9. $85; 10 thru 19. $75; 20 thru 23. $65; 24. $50; 25 and 26. $35.

Millhiser, Marlys
1. $25; 2 thru 4. $20; 5. $15.

Milne, A.A.
1. $500; 2 thru 13. $375; 14. $750; 15 thru 18. $375; 19. $450; 20 thru 22. $375; 23. $1,200; 24 and 25. $375; 26. $525; 27. $375; 28. $1,000; 29 and 30. $375; 31. $900; 32 thru 35. $325; 36 and 37. $275; 38. $225; 39. $375; 40 thru 57. $225; 58 thru 63. $175; 64 thru 66. $125; 67 and 68. $75.

Mitchell, Gladys
1 and 2. $85; 3 thru 26. $65; 27 thru 48. $60; 49 thru 62. $50; 63 thru 79. $40.

Mitchell, Margaret
1. $750; 2. $25.

Moore, Doris Langley
1. $65; 2. $45; 3 thru 9. $40; 10 thru 12. $35; 13 thru 18. $30; 19. $25; 20. $35.

Morland, Nigel
1 and 2. $175; 3 thru 34. $125; 35 thru 49. $115; 50 thru 72. $100; 73 thru 93. $90; 94 thru 98. $75; 99 and 100. $40; 101. $35.

Morrissey, J.L.
1 thru 5. $35.

Murray, Frances
1. $35; 2 thru 6. $25; 7 and 8. $20.

Neihardt, John G.
1. $375; 2. $125; 3. $900; 4 thru 10. $125; 11 thru 15. $110; 16 and 17. $100; 18 and 19. $85; 20 and 21. $75; 22. $65; 23 and 24. $50; 25 and 26. $35.

Newton, D.B.
1. $45; 2 thru 4. $35; 5 thru 22. $30; 23 thru 48. $25; 49 thru 64. $20; 65 thru 67. $15.

Nickson, Arthur
1. $45; 2 thru 11. $35; 12 thru 54. $30.

Nichols, John
1. $75; 2. $60; 3 thru 6. $50; 7. $35; 8. $25.

Nicole, Christopher
1. $75; 2. $60; 3 thru 20. $50; 21 thru 50. $40.

Niven, Frederick
1. $75; 2 thru 16. $60; 17 thru 24. $50; 25 thru 36. $40; 37 thru 40. $35.

Nolan, Frederick
1. $40; 2 thru 6. $35; 7 thru 34. $30; 35 thru 37. $25.

Norris, Frank
1. $1,850; 2 thru 4. $300; 5. $750; 6 and 7. $300; 8. $225; 9 thru 12. $125; 13 thru 15. $100; 16. $75; 17. $65; 18 and 19. $45; 20. $35.

Nye, Nelson
1 and 2. $65; 3 thru 17. $45; 18 thru 43. $40; 44 thru 95. $35; 96 thru 133. $30; 134 thru 139. $25; 140 thru 143. $20.

Obets, Bob
1. $35; 2. $25.

O'Conner, Jack
1. $150; 2 thru 15. $125; 16 thru 19. $100.

O'Connor, Richard
1. $75; 2 and 3. $65; 4 thru 7. $40; 8. $65; 9 thru 12. $40; 13. $65; 14. $35; 15 and 16. $65; 17 thru 19. $35; 20. $65; 21 thru 26. $35; 27. $65; 28. $35; 29. $65; 30 and 31. $35; 32. $65; 33. $35; 34 and 35. $65; 36 and 37. $35; 38. $65; 39. $35; 40 and 41. $65; 42 thru 44. $25; 45 and 46. $65; 47 thru 52. $25; 53. $45.

Olsen, T.V.
1. $45; 2. $35; 3 thru 22. $30; 23 thru 39. $25; 40 and 41. $20.

Onstott, Kyle
1 thru 4. $25.

O'Rourke, Frank
1. $50; 2 thru 5. $40; 6 thru 45. $35; 46 thru 66. $30; 67 thru 69. $25.

Ostenso, Martha
1. $65; 2 thru 6. $50; 7 thru 15. $40; 16 and 17. $35; 18. $25.

Overholser, Wayne D.
1. $65; 2. $50; 3 thru 41. $45; 42 thru 85. $40; 86 thru 98. $35; 99 thru 101. $30.

Ovstedal, Barbara
1. $50; 2 thru 18. $40; 19 thru 21. $35.

Palmer, John Leslie
1. $90; 2 thru 10. $75; 11 thru 21. $65; 22 thru 60. $55; 61 thru 63. $45.

Patten, Lewis B.
1. $65; 2 thru 12. $50; 13 thru 25. $45; 26 thru 64. $40; 65 thru 100. $35; 101. $25.

Pattullo, George
1. $65; 2. $50; 3. $45; 4 thru 6. $40; 7. $35; 8 thru 13. $30.

Pendower, Jacques
1. $125; 2 thru 12. $85; 13 thru 16. $75; 17 thru 60. $65; 61 thru 102. $50; 103 thru 107. $40.

Perry, George Sessions
1. $45; 2 thru 6. $35; 7 thru 9. $30; 10 thru 12. $25.

Pocock, Roger
1. $175; 2 thru 5. $125; 6 thru 9. $110; 10 thru 17. $100; 18. $85; 19. $65.

Portis, Charles
1 and 2. $75; 3. $50.

Potter, Margaret
1. $45; 2 thru 16. $35; 17 thru 34. $30; 35 thru 37. $25.

Powell, James
1. $35; 2 and 3. $25; 4 thru 6. $20.

Prebble, John
1. $50; 2 and 3. $40; 4 thru 13. $35; 14 thru 17. $30; 18 thru 21. $25.

Prescott, John
1. $45; 2 thru 7. $35; 8 thru 11. $30.

Pritchard, John Wallace
1. $65; 2 thru 5. $45; 6 thru 12. $35; 13. $25.

Purdum, Herbert R.
1. $35; 2. $25.

Queen, Ellery
1. $650; 2. $375; 3 thru 11. $150; 12. $200; 13 thru 16. $150; 17. $200; 18 thru 25. $150; 26 thru 29. $125; 30 thru 45. $110; 46 thru 57. $100; 58 and 59. $85.

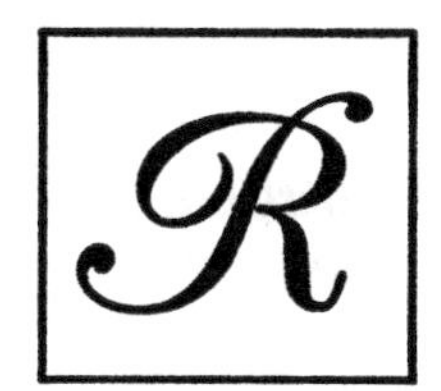

Raine, William MacLeod
1. $175; 2 thru 17. $150; 18 thru 37. $125; 38 thru 73. $100; 74 thru 85. $85; 86 thru 109. $75; 110 and 111. $65; 112 and 113. $35.

Rathborne, St. George
1. $225; 3 thru 35. $150; 36 thru 89. $140; 90 thru 128. $130; 129 thru 177. $120; 178 thru 181. $110; 182 thru 187. $100; 188. $175.

Reese, John
1. $65; 2 thru 5. $40; 6 thru 13. $35; 14 thru 37. $30; 38 thru 41. $25.

Repp, Ed
1 and 2. $65; 3 thru 6. $50; 7 and 8. $40; 9 thru 14. $35.

Rhodes, Eugene Manlove
1. $225; 2 thru 4. $175; 5 and 6. $150; 7. $200; 8 thru 14. $125; 15. $200; 16. $75; 17. $65; 18 thru 20. $35.

Richmond, Roe
1. $45; 2 thru 11. $35; 12 thru 16. $30; 17. $25; 18 thru 29. $20.

Richter, Conrad
1. $350; 2. $525; 3. $325; 4. $300; 5 thru 7. $225; 8 thru 10. $175; 11 thru 14. $125; 15 thru 21. $100; 22. $65.

Rigsby, Howard
1. $50; 2 thru 16. $35; 17 thru 20. $25.

Roan, Tom
1 and 2. $40; 3 thru 8. $30; 9 thru 20. $25.

Robertson, Frank C.
1. $100; 2 thru 14. $85; 15 thru 92. $75; 93 thru 101. $65; 102 thru 127. $55; 128. $45; 129. $75; 130 thru 147. $45.

Roderus, Frank
1 and 2. $35; 3 thru 8. $25; 9 thru 12. $20.

Ross, Sinclair
1. $45; 2. $35; 3. $30; 4 and 5. $25; 6. $20.

Ross, Zola
1. $65; 2 thru 4. $50; 5 thru 25. $45; 26 thru 29. $35.

Rowland, Donald S.
1. $85; 2 thru 165. $65; 166 thru 317. $55; 318 thru 330. $35; 331 thru 340. $30; 341 thru 349. $25.

Rushing, Jane Gilmore
1. $35; 2 thru 5. $25; 6. $20.

Russell, Charles M.
1. $425; 2 thru 5. $375; 6. $225; 7. $125; 8. $85.

Ryan, Marah Ellis
1. $85; 2 thru 8. $65; 9 thru 14. $55; 15 thru 17. $45; 18 and 19. $35.

Sabatini, Rafael
1 and 2. $100; 3 thru 8. $75; 9 thru 19. $65; 20. $125; 21. $50; 22. $75; 23 thru 32. $50; 33 thru 49. $40; 50 thru 52. $35; 53 thru 55. $30.

Saberhagen, Fred
1. $85; 2 thru 6. $65; 7 thru 20. $55; 21 and 22. $45.

Sachs, Marilyn
1 and 2. $45; 3 thru 5. $35; 6 thru 12. $25.

Sale, Richard
1. $45; 2 thru 9. $35; 10 thru 12. $25; 13 thru 15. $20.

Salkey, Andrew
1. $50; 2 thru 10. $35; 11 thru 17. $25.

Sallis, James
1 and 2. $35.

Sanders, Dorothy Lucy
1 and 2. $55; 3 thru 15. $40; 16 thru 35. $35; 36 thru 43. $30.

Sanders, Lawrence
1. $65; 2 and 3. $125; 4. $100; 5. $85; 6 thru 9. $75; 10. $65; 11. $50.

Sandoz, Mari
1. $150; 2 thru 4. $125; 5. $100; 6 thru 12. $85; 13 thru 18. $75; 19. $125; 20. $225; 21. $125; 22 and 23. $85.

Santee, Ross
1. $300; 2. $225; 3 thru 6. $175; 7 thru 9. $125; 10 thru 12. $100; 13. $75.

Sarban, John W.
1. $65; 2 and 3. $50; 4. $35.

Sargent, Pamela
1 thru 3. $25; 4 and 5. $20.

Saville, Malcolm
1 thru 3. $45; 4 thru 30. $40; 31. $80; 32 thru 44. $40; 45 thru 61. $35; 62 thru 66. $30.

Sawyer, Ruth
1. $65; 2 thru 6. $50; 7 thru 10. $45; 11 thru 22. $40; 23 thru 29. $35; 30 thru 35. $30.

Saunders, Hilary Adam St. George
1. $135; 2 thru 7. $100; 8 thru 41. $90; 42 thru 45. $80.

Saxton, Josephine
1. $65; 2 thru 4. $50; 5. $35.

Sayers, Dorothy L.
1. $600; 2. $275; 3 thru 8. $225; 9 thru 32. $200; 33. $165; 34. $85; 35. $65; 36 and 37. $45.

Sayers, James Denson
1. $100; 2 thru 15. $85; 16 thru 22. $65; 23. $45.

Scarborough, Dorothy
1. $75; 2. $55; 3 thru 7. $45; 8 and 9. $35.

Scarry, Richard
1. $85; 2 thru 4. $65; 5 thru 40. $55; 41 thru 68. $45.

Schachner, Nat
1. $45; 2 thru 5. $35; 6. $25.

Schaefer, Jack
1. $65; 2 thru 8. $50; 9 thru 18. $40; 19. $35.

Scherf, Margaret
1. $65; 2 and 3. $50; 4 thru 9. $40; 10 thru 19. $30; 20 thru 27. $25; 28 thru 32. $20.

Schlee, Ann
1. $25; 2 thru 5. $20.

Schlein, Miriam
1. $45; 2 thru 33. $35; 34 thru 47. $30; 48 thru 56. $25.

Schmidt, Stanley
1. $85; 2. $65; 3. $50.

Schmitz, James H.
1. $85; 2 thru 6. $65; 7 thru 10. $50; 11. $35.

Scortia, Thomas N.
1. $65; 2. $50; 3 thru 6. $35; 7. $35; 8. $25.

Scott, R.T.M.
1. $65; 2 thru 5. $50; 6 and 7. $40; 8 and 9. $35.

Seale, Sara
1. $60; 2 thru 11. $45; 12 thru 32. $40; 33 thru 47. $35; 48 thru 50. $30; 51. $25.

Searls, Hank
1. $40; 2 thru 6. $30; 7 thru 10. $25; 11. $20.

Seed, Jenny
1. $35; 2 thru 11. $25; 12 thru 22. $20.

Seeley, Mabel
1. $50; 2 thru 5. $40; 6. $35; 7 thru 10. $30.

Seelye, John
1. $35; 2 thru 4. $25.

Seifert, Elizabeth
1. $60; 2 thru 16. $45; 17 thru 54. $40; 55 thru 76. $35; 77 thru 97. $30.

Selden, George
1. $45; 2. $35; 3 thru 9. $30; 10 and 11. $25.

Sellings, Arthur
1. $60; 2 thru 8. $45; 9. $35.

Seltzer, Charles Alden
1. $125; 2. $100; 3 thru 12. $90; 13 thru 32. $80; 33 thru 45. $70; 46 thru 55. $50.

Selwyn, Francis
1. $45; 2 thru 5. $35.

Senarens, Luis P.
1 thru 4. $350; 5 thru 10. $275; 11 thru 191. $250; 192 thru 218. $225.

Sendak, Maurice
1. $85; 2. $60; 3. $50; 4. $80; 5 and 6. $50; 7 thru 10. $40; 11 and 12. $35.

Seredy, Kate
1. $75; 2 thru 6. $60; 7. $50; 8 thru 10. $40; 11 and 12. $35.

Serling, Rod
1. $65; 2 and 3. $45; 4. $75; 5 thru 7. $45; 8 thru 11. $35.

Serviss, Garrett P.
1. $350; 2. $500; 3. $375; 4 and 5. $225; 6. $175; 7. $130; 8. $65.

Seton, Anya
1. $75; 2. $60; 3 thru 8. $50; 9 thru 11. $40; 12. $35; 13. $30.

Seton, Ernest Thompson
1. $375; 2. $325; 3 thru 9. $275; 10 thru 14. $225; 15 thru 18. $200; 19 thru 25. $175; 26 thru 29. $150; 30 thru 36. $125; 37. $100; 38 and 39. $75; 40. $65; 41. $50.

Seuss, Dr.
1. $265; 2 thru 4. $225; 5. $175; 6 thru 8. $150; 9 thru 19. $125; 20 thru 37. $100; 38 thru 54. $85.

Severn, David
1. $60; 2 and 3. $45; 4 thru 22. $40; 23 thru 26. $35; 27 and 28. $30.

Sewell, Helen
1. $75; 2 thru 8. $60; 9. $45.

Shannon, Monica
1. $45; 2. $35; 3 thru 6. $30.

Sharkey, Jack
1 and 2. $45; 3. $35; 4 and 5. $25.

Sharmat, Marjorie Weinman
1. $35; 2. $25; 3 thru 25. $20.

Sharp, Margery
1. $90; 2 thru 11. $75; 12 thru 17. $65; 18 thru 28. $55; 29 thru 38. $45.

Shaver, Richard S.
1. $65.

Shaw, Bob
1. $65; 2 thru 4. $50; 5 thru 16. $35.

Shaw, Felicity
1. $50; 2. $35; 3 thru 15. $25.

Sheckley, Robert
1. $65; 2 thru 5. $50; 6 thru 21. $40; 22 thru 30. $35.

Shellabarger, Samuel
1. $100; 2. $50; 3. $75; 4 thru 14. $65; 15 and 16. $50; 17 thru 22. $40.

Shelley, John L.
1. $35; 2 thru 10. $25; 11. $20.

Sherriff, R.C.
1 and 2. $50.

Shiras, Wilmar H.
1. $45; 2. $35.

Short, Luke
1. $125; 2 thru 22. $75; 23 thru 50. $60; 51 thru 62. $50; 63 thru 68. $40.

Shrake, Edwin
1. $60; 2 and 3. $45; 4 thru 6. $35.

Shute, Nevil
1. $125; 2 and 3. $75; 4 thru 12. $65; 13 thru 20. $55; 21. $85; 22 thru 26. $55; 27 and 28. $45.

Siller, Van
1 thru 3. $50; 4 thru 8. $40; 9 thru 13. $35; 14 thru 23. $30; 24 thru 27. $25.

Silverberg, Robert
1. $75; 2 thru 14. $50; 15 thru 92. $45; 93 thru 134. $40; 135. $35.

Simak, Clifford D.
1. $125; 2 thru 8. $75; 9 thru 25. $65; 26 thru 35. $50; 36 thru 38. $35; 39 and 40. $25.

Simon, Roger L.
1. $35; 2 thru 5. $25.

Simpson, Helen
1 and 2. $65; 3 thru 6. $50; 7 thru 22. $40.

Sims, George
1. $85; 2 and 3. $65; 4 thru 8. $50; 9 thru 12. $40.

Sinclair, Olga
1 and 2. $45; 3 thru 5. $35; 6 thru 16. $30; 17 and 18. $25.

Sinclair, Upton
1. $225; 2. $175; 3 thru 40. $150; 41 thru 65. $125; 66 thru 111. $100; 112 thru 129. $85; 130 thru 135. $65; 136. $50.

Singer, Isaac Bashevis
1. $275; 2 and 3. $225; 4 thru 16. $200; 17 thru 20. $175; 21 thru 24. $150; 25 thru 27. $125; 28 thru 32. $100.

Sladek, John
1. $125; 2 thru 5. $100; 6 thru 9. $85; 10 and 11. $65; 12 and 13. $50.

Slaughter, Frank G.
1. $85; 2 thru 4. $60; 5 thru 40. $50; 41 thru 60. $40; 61 thru 70. $35; 71 and 72. $25.

Slesar, Henry
1. $50; 2 thru 6. $35; 7. $25.

Sloane, William M.
1 thru 3. $50; 4 thru 11. $40; 12. $35; 13. $25.

Slobodkin, Louis
1 and 2. $75; 3 thru 27. $60; 28 thru 40. $50; 41 and 42. $40.

Slobodkina, Esphyr
1. $50; 2 thru 8. $40; 9 thru 13. $35; 14. $25.

Smith, Clark Ashton
1. $275; 2 thru 6. $225; 7 and 8. $175; 9. $275; 10. $160; 11. $125; 12. $325; 13. $375; 14. $300; 15 and 16. $325; 17. $100; 18 thru 22. $85.

Smith, E.E.
1. $125; 2. $135; 3. $125; 4 thru 16. $110; 17 thru 19. $65.

Smith, George H.
1 thru 3. $35; 4 thru 17. $25; 18 thru 24. $20.

Smith, George O.
1. $85; 2. $65; 3 thru 12. $50; 13 thru 16. $35.

Smith, Joan
1 and 2. $35; 3 thru 9. $25; 10 thru 16. $20.

Smith, Shelley
1. $50; 2 thru 6. $40; 7 thru 16. $35; 17. $30; 18 and 19. $25.

Snedeker, Caroline Dale
1. $65; 2 and 3. $50; 4 thru 8. $45; 9 thru 11. $40; 12 and 13. $35; 14. $30; 15. $25.

Snow, Charles H.
1. $125; 2 thru 179. $95; 180 thru 338. $85; 339 thru 419. $75.

Snyder, Zilpha Keatley
1. $40; 2 thru 6. $30; 7 thru 14. $25.

Sobol, Donald J.
1. $35; 2 and 3. $30; 4 thru 10. $25; 11 thru 14. $20.

Sohl, Jerry
1. $65; 2 thru 10. $50; 11. $45; 12. $40; 13 thru 23. $35.

Sorensen, Virginia
1. $50; 2 thru 4. $40; 5 thru 10. $35; 11 thru 13. $30; 14 thru 16. $25.

Speare, Elizabeth George
1. $35; 2. $30; 3 thru 6. $25.

Spearman, Frank H.
1. $150; 2 thru 7. $100; 8. $150; 9 thru 11. $85; 12. $75; 13 thru 16. $70; 17 thru 20. $65.

Spence, Bill
1. $60; 2 thru 15. $45; 16 thru 27. $35; 28 thru 32. $25.

Sperry, Armstrong
1. $60; 2 thru 13. $45; 14 thru 17. $40; 18 thru 21. $35.

Spicer, Bart
1. $65; 2 thru 16. $50; 17 thru 21. $40; 22 and 23. $30.

Spillane, Mickey
1. $225; 2 thru 7. $65; 8 thru 22. $50; 23 thru 25. $40.

Spinrad, Norman
1. $100; 2 thru 4. $75; 5 thru 13. $60; 14. $50.

Sprigg, Christopher St. John
1. $75; 2 thru 6. $85; 7 and 8. $45; 9 thru 13. $65.

Spykman, E.C.
1. $40; 2 and 3. $30; 4. $25; 5. $20.

Stableford, Brian M.
1. $65; 2 thru 25. $45; 26. $35.

Stafford, Jean
1. $75; 2. $65; 3 thru 7. $50; 8 thru 13. $40.

Starrett, Vincent
1. $450; 2. $125; 3. $150; 4. $1,500; 5. $75; 6. $150; 7 thru 10. $125; 11. $225; 12. $125; 13. $300; 14 thru 17. $225; 18 thru 23. $175; 24. $75; 25 and 26. $125; 27 and 28. $100; 29 and 30. $125; 31 thru 35. $100; 36. $150; 37 and 38. $75.

Stasheff, Christopher
1. $45; 2. $35; 3. $25.

Steel, Danielle
1. $50; 2 thru 5. $35; 6 thru 15. $25.

Steele, Mary Q.
1. $45; 2 thru 7. $35; 8 thru 15. $25.

Steele, William O.
1. $65; 2 thru 20. $55; 21 thru 28. $45; 29 thru 35. $35.

Steelman, Robert J.
1. $40; 2 and 3. $30; 4 and 5. $25; 6 thru 18. $20.

Steen, Marguerite
1. $75; 2 thru 4. $60; 5 thru 28. $55; 29 thru 32. $50; 33 thru 41. $45; 42 and 43. $40; 44 and 45. $35.

Stegner, Wallace
1. $65; 2 thru 6. $50; 7 thru 11. $45; 12 thru 15. $40; 16. $35; 17. $45; 18. $75; 19 and 20. $35; 21 and 22. $30.

Stein, Aaron Marc
1. $125; 2 thru 15. $85; 16 thru 64. $75; 65 thru 88. $65; 89 thru 109. $55; 110. $45.

Steinbeck, John
1. $5,250; 2. $1,875; 3. $1,275; 4. $1,125; 5. $450; 6. $2,225; 7. $450; 8. $1,125; 9. $265; 10 and 11. $675; 12. $265; 13. $375; 14. $150; 15. $190; 16 and 17. $85; 18. $225; 19. $85; 20 and 21. $190; 22. $400; 23. $375; 24. $190; 25. $75; 26. $130; 27. $75; 28 and 29. $225; 30. $65; 31. $110; 32 and 33. $100; 34. $110; 35. $85; 36 and 37. $65.

Steptoe, John
1. $30; 2 thru 6. $20.

Stevens, James
1. $125; 2 thru 4. $100; 5. $85; 6. $65; 7 and 8. $50.

Stevenson, Anne
1. $40; 2. $30; 3 thru 7. $25; 8. $20.

Stevenson, Florence
1. $45; 2. $35; 3 thru 27. $30; 28 thru 30. $25; 31 thru 34. $20; 35 thru 38. $25.

Stewart, J.I.M.
1. $100; 2 thru 13. $85; 14 thru 43. $75; 44 thru 66. $65; 67 thru 88. $55.

Stewart, Mary
1. $75; 2 thru 4. $60; 5 thru 11. $50; 12. $85; 13 thru 17. $40.

Stine, Hank
1. $35; 2 and 3. $25.

Stockton, Frank R.
1. $600; 2. $350; 3 thru 6. $150; 7. $300; 8 and 9. $225; 10 thru 17. $125; 18 thru 41. $100; 42 thru 48. $85; 49. $65.

Stoker, Bram
1. $275; 2. $350; 3. $125; 4 thru 8. $350; 9. $1,800; 10. $275; 11 thru 17. $225; 18. $100; 19. $150; 20. $225; 21 and 22. $50; 23. $45.

Stolz, Mary
1. $40; 2 thru 19. $30; 20 thru 36. $25; 37 thru 43. $20.

Stong, Phil
1. $50; 2 thru 28. $40; 29 thru 42. $35.

Stout, Rex
1. $275; 2 thru 4. $225; 5. $650; 6 thru 23. $225; 24 thru 50. $175; 51 thru 65. $150; 66. $100; 67. $85; 68 and 69. $75.

Strange, John Stephen
1. $100; 2 and 3. $85; 4 thru 18. $75; 19 thru 23. $65; 24 thru 32. $50; 33. $40; 34. $25.

Strete, Craig
1. $150; 2. $85; 3. $65.

Stribling, T.S.
1. $275; 2 thru 9. $225; 10 thru 15. $100; 16. $45.

Sturgeon, Theodore
1. $275; 2 thru 13. $225; 14 thru 19. $175; 20. $75; 21 thru 24. $125; 25 thru 32. $100.

Sublette, C.M.
1. $45; 2. $35; 3 and 4. $30; 5. $25.

Suddaby, Donald
1. $50; 2. $35; 3 thru 11. $30; 12 thru 15. $25.

Swarthout, Glendon
1. $65; 2. $50; 3 thru 10. $35; 11 thru 17. $30; 18. $25.

Symons, Julian
1. $125; 2. $85; 3 thru 19. $75; 20 thru 36. $65; 37 thru 47. $50.

Tall, Stephen
1. $45; 2. $35; 3. $25.

Tate, Joan
1 thru 33. $35; 34 thru 69. $25.

Tate, Peter
1. $35; 2 thru 5. $25; 6. $20.

Tattersall, Jill
1. $40; 2 thru 5. $30; 6 thru 13. $25; 14. $20.

Taylor, Phoebe Atwood
1. $85; 2 thru 27. $65; 28 thru 33. $55.

Taylor, Robert Lewis
1. $85; 2 and 3. $65; 4 thru 8. $50; 9 and 10. $40; 11. $35.

Taylor, Sydney
1. $35; 2 and 3. $30; 4 thru 7. $25; 8. $20.

Taylor, Theodore
1. $40; 2. $30; 3 and 4. $25; 5 thru 9. $20.

Telfair, Richard
1 thru 6. $35; 7 thru 11. $25.

Tenn, William
1. $65; 2 and 3. $50; 4 thru 8. $35.

Tennant, Emma
1. $45; 2 thru 7. $35; 8 and 9. $25.

Tevis, Walter
1. $35; 2. $25; 3 and 4. $20.

Tey, Josephine
1 and 2. $85; 3 thru 6. $65; 7 thru 13. $50.

Thane, Elswyth
1. $65; 2 thru 4. $50; 5 thru 13. $45; 14 thru 24. $40; 25 thru 28. $35; 29. $25.

Thayer, Lee
1. $110; 2 and 3. $95; 4 thru 14. $85; 15 thru 50. $75; 51 thru 57. $65; 58 thru 75. $55; 76 thru 79. $45.

Thomas, Ross
1. $85; 2 thru 6. $60; 7 thru 20. $45.

Thomason, Jr., John W.
1. $50; 2 and 3. $40; 4 thru 8. $35; 9 and 10. $25.

Thompson, Thomas
1 and 2. $45; 3 thru 13. $35; 14 thru 17. $25.

Thomson, Basil
1 and 2. $175; 3 and 4. $150; 5 and 6. $125; 7 thru 11. $110; 12 thru 31. $100.

Thomson, June
1. $25; 2 thru 7. $20.

Thorpe, Kay
1 thru 4. $35; 5 thru 28. $25; 29 thru 32. $20.

Thorpe, Sylvia
1. $50; 2 thru 9. $45; 10 thru 19. $40; 20 thru 28. $35; 29. $25.

Thurber, James
1. $325; 2 thru 4. $265; 5. $250; 6 thru 17. $225; 18 thru 21. $175; 22 thru 25. $150; 26 thru 28. $125.

Tidyman, Ernest
1 and 2. $50; 3 thru 15. $35.

Tippette, Giles
1. $35; 2 thru 9. $30; 10 thru 15. $25.

Titus, Eve
1. $45; 2 thru 4. $35; 5 thru 12. $30; 13 thru 18. $25.

Todd, Barbara Euphan
1. $65; 2 thru 5. $55; 6 thru 18. $50; 19 thru 30. $45; 31 thru 34. $40; 35 and 36. $35.

Tolbert, Frank X.
1. $25; 2 thru 4. $35; 5. $40; 6. $25; 7. $20.

Tolkien, J.R.R.
1. $300; 2. $150; 3. $225; 4. $150; 5. $125; 6 thru 8. $350; 9. $225; 10 thru 13. $125; 14 thru 17. $100.

Tomalin, Ruth
1. $60; 2. $45; 3 thru 8. $40; 9 thru 11. $35; 12 thru 15. $25.

Tompkins, Walker A.
1. $75; 2 thru 15. $60; 16 thru 35. $50; 36 thru 42. $45; 43 thru 46. $40; 47 and 48. $35.

Torday, Ursula
1. $85; 2 and 3. $65; 4 thru 22. $40; 23 thru 48. $35; 49 thru 75. $30; 76 thru 81. $25.

Townsend, John Rowe
1. $45; 2 thru 9. $35; 10 thru 15. $30; 16 thru 19. $25.

Train, Arthur
1. $135; 2 thru 5. $100; 6 thru 11. $90; 12 thru 28. $80; 29 thru 46. $70; 47. $60; 48. $50; 49. $40.

Tranter, Nigel
1. $65; 2 thru 4. $50; 5 thru 8. $45; 9 thru 48. $35; 49 thru 58. $30; 59. $85; 60 thru 77. $30; 78 and 79. $25; 80. $85; 81 thru 91. $25; 92 thru 95. $20.

Travers, P.L.
1. $225; 2. $165; 3 thru 6. $45; 7. $100; 8. $45; 9. $65; 10. $35; 11. $50; 12 and 13. $25; 14. $35.

Treadgold, Mary
1 and 2. $50; 3. $45; 4 thru 6. $35; 7 thru 15. $25; 16. $20.

Trease, Geoffrey
1. $65; 2 thru 20. $50; 21 thru 45. $45; 46 thru 60. $40; 61 thru 76. $35.

Treat, Lawrence
1. $85; 2 thru 8. $60; 9 thru 15. $50; 16 and 17. $45; 18 and 19. $40; 20. $35.

Treece, Henry
1. $100; 2 thru 9. $75; 10 thru 36. $65; 37 thru 67. $55; 68. $45.

Trench, John
1. $45; 2 and 3. $35; 4 thru 6. $25.

Tresselt, Alvin
1. $100; 2 thru 6. $75; 7 thru 18. $65; 19 thru 37. $55; 38 thru 51. $45.

Trevor, Elleston
1. $90; 2. $100; 3 thru 6. $75; 7 thru 55. $65; 56 thru 72. $55; 73 thru 88. $45.

Trevor, Meriol
1. $45; 2 thru 14. $35; 15 thru 21. $30; 22 thru 31. $25.

Trimble, Louis
1. $85; 2 thru 5. $75; 6 thru 38. $65; 39 thru 57. $55; 58 thru 65. $45.

Tripp, Miles
1. $65; 2. $50; 3 thru 14. $40; 15 thru 23. $30.

Trollope, Joanna
1. $25; 2 thru 6. $20.

Tubb, E.C.
1 and 2. $75; 3 thru 47. $60; 48 thru 73. $50; 74 thru 120. $40; 121 thru 123. $25.

Tucker, Wilson
1. $90; 2 thru 4. $65; 5 thru 17. $55; 18 thru 21. $45; 22 thru 24. $35.

Tudor, Tasha
1. $125; 2 thru 7. $75; 8 thru 15. $65; 16 thru 18. $55; 19. $45.

Tunis, John R.
1. $50; 2 thru 18. $40; 19 thru 28. $35; 29 thru 31. $30; 32. $20.

Turkle, Brinton
1. $45; 2 thru 5. $35; 6 thru 9. $25.

Turner, Philip
1 thru 10. $25; 11 thru 17. $20.

Tuttle, W.C.
1. $150; 2 thru 24. $95; 25 thru 45. $85; 46 thru 65. $75; 66 thru 87. $65; 88 thru 90. $45.

Twain, Mark
1. $7,500; 2. $1,200; 3. $500; 4 and 5. $375; 6. $650; 7. $475; 8. $375; 9. $2,000; 10. $50; 11. $650; 12. $3,200; 13. $750; 14. $1,300; 15. $575; 16. $375; 17. $750; 18. $1,000; 19. $650; 20. $375; 21. $325; 22. $400; 23. $750; 24. $575; 25. $1,000; 26. $500; 27 and 28. $250; 29. $850; 30. $650; 31. $475; 32. $300; 33. $225; 34. $375; 35. $175; 36 and 37. $375; 38. $500; 39 and 40. $375; 41. $475; 42. $375; 43. $400; 44. $375; 45 and 46. $250; 47. $225; 48. $300; 49. $275; 50. $325; 51 thru 53. $275; 54. $225; 55. $250; 56 thru 58. $225; 59. $750; 60. $225; 61. $475; 62. $250; 63. $225; 64. $350; 65 thru 70. $325; 71. $450; 72 thru 75. $275; 76 thru 84. $225;

85 thru 91. $200; 92. $800; 93 thru 96. $175; 97. $1,200; 98. $175; 99 thru 106. $150; 107 thru 137. $125; 138 thru 149. $100.

Tyre, Nedra
1. $45; 2 thru 5. $35; 6 thru 8. $30; 9. $25.

Uchida, Yoshiko
1. $75; 2 thru 7. $55; 8 thru 16. $45; 17 thru 22. $35.

Ude, Wayne
1. $35; 2. $25.

Udry, Janice
1. $45; 2 thru 4. $35; 5 thru 19. $30; 20 thru 23. $25.

Uhnak, Dorothy
1. $50; 2 and 3. $45; 4 thru 6. $35.

Underwood, Michael
1. $55; 2 thru 6. $45; 7 thru 18. $40; 19 thru 30. $35; 31. $25.

Ungerer, Tomi
1. $40; 2 thru 5. $35; 6 thru 18. $30; 19 thru 21. $25.

Unwin, Nora S.
1. $45; 2. $35; 3 thru 5. $30; 6 thru 9. $25; 10. $20.

Upfield, Arthur W.
1. $375; 2. $225; 3 thru 16. $200; 17 thru 35. $175; 36 thru 43. $150.

Upton, Bertha
1. $225; 2 thru 6. $175; 7 thru 11. $150; 12 thru 15. $125.

Vaizey, Mrs. George de Horne
1. $100; 2 and 3. $65; 4 thru 17. $55; 18 thru 33. $45.

Vance, Jack
1. $175; 2 thru 7. $125; 8. $100; 9. $85; 10 thru 35. $65; 36 thru 54. $45.

Vance, Louis Joseph
1. $95; 2 thru 6. $75; 7 thru 19. $65; 20 thru 33. $55; 34 thru 41. $45.

Vance, William E.
1. $60; 2 thru 7. $45; 8 thru 16. $40; 17. $30; 18 thru 20. $25.

Van Dine, S.S.
1. $125; 2 thru 9. $45; 10. $375; 11. $350; 12. $325; 13. $300; 14. $275; 15. $250; 16. $225; 17. $200; 18. $175; 19 thru 22. $125; 23. $85.

Van Slyke, Helen
1. $35; 2 thru 10. $25; 11 and 12. $20.

Van Stockum, Hilda
1. $65; 2 thru 7. $50; 8 thru 10. $40; 11 and 12. $35; 13 thru 19. $30; 20 thru 22. $25.

van Vogt, A.E.
1. $275; 2 thru 5. $175; 6 thru 24. $150; 25 thru 41. $125; 42 thru 69. $100; 70. $85.

Varley, John
1. $50; 2 thru 4. $35; 5 and 6. $25.

Verney, John
1. $65; 2 thru 4. $50; 5. $45; 6 thru 11. $40; 12. $35.

Vernon, Roger Lee
1. $45; 2. $35.

Verrill, A. Hyatt
1. $110; 2 thru 28. $85; 29 thru 49. $75; 50 thru 71. $65; 72. $50; 73 thru 75. $45; 76. $35.

Veryan, Patricia
1. $30; 2. $25; 3 thru 7. $20.

Vickers, Roy C.
1. $125; 2 thru 17. $95; 18 thru 60. $85; 61 thru 75. $75; 76. $45.

Vidal, Gore
1. $225; 2 and 3. $165; 4. $150; 5. $125; 6 thru 11. $100; 12 and 13. $75; 14 thru 24. $65; 25 thru 31. $50.

Vinge, Joan D.
1 and 2. $45; 3. $35; 4. $25.

Vining, Elizabeth Gray
1. $75; 2 and 3. $60; 4 thru 11. $55; 12 thru 17. $50; 18 thru 25. $45; 26 thru 29. $40.

Viorst, Judith
1. $60; 2 thru 8. $45; 9 thru 18. $35.

Vonnegut, Jr., Kurt
1. $350; 2 and 3. $175; 4 thru 7. $165; 8 thru 12. $150; 13. $125; 14. $100.

Waber, Bernard
1. $40; 3 thru 12. $30; 13 thru 20. $35.

Wade, Henry
1. $85; 2 thru 4. $65; 5 thru 17. $55; 18. $45; 19 thru 24. $35.

Wade, Robert
1. $100; 2 thru 6. $75; 7 thru 31. $65; 32 thru 45. $55; 46 thru 53. $45.

Wagoner, David
1. $75; 2 thru 5. $60; 7 thru 11. $50; 12 thru 23. $45; 24 and 25. $35.

Wahl, Jan
1 thru 4. $45; 5 thru 18. $35; 19 thru 56. $25.

Wainwright, John
1 and 2. $65; 3 thru 11. $50; 12 thru 51. $40.

Waldo, Dave
1. $45; 2 thru 11. $35.

Walker, David
1. $45; 2 thru 5. $35; 6 thru 15. $30; 16 thru 19. $25.

Wallace, Edgar
1. $225; 2 thru 5. $190; 6. $175; 7 thru 12. $165; 13 thru 47. $150; 48 thru 161. $125; 162 thru 195. $100; 196 and 197. $65; 198. $50; 199 and 200. $35.

Walling, R.A.J.
1. $110; 2 and 3. $65; 4 thru 7. $85; 8 thru 52. $75; 53 thru 55. $50.

Walsh, J.M.
1 and 2. $100; 3 thru 19. $85; 20 thru 71. $75; 72 thru 83. $65; 84 thru 89. $50.

Walsh, Sheila
1. $35; 2 thru 4. $25; 5 thru 7. $20.

Walsh, Thomas
1. $60; 2 thru 4. $45; 5 thru 11. $35.

Walters, Hugh
1. $65; 2 thru 4. $50; 5 thru 18. $40; 19 thru 27. $35.

Wambaugh, Joseph
1. $125; 2 and 3. $85; 4. $75; 5. $65.

Wandrei, Donald
1. $300; 2. $175; 3. $150; 4. $125; 5 and 6. $110.

Warren, Charles Marquis
1. $35; 2 and 3. $25.

Warriner, Thurman
1. $65; 2 thru 10. $50; 11 thru 19. $40; 20. $35.

Waterloo, Stanley
1. $175; 2 thru 8. $135; 9 thru 11. $125; 12. $100.

Waters, Frank
1. $100; 2 thru 8. $85; 9 thru 11. $75; 12. $65; 13 thru 18. $45; 19 and 20. $35.

Watkins, William Jon
1. $65; 2. $50; 3 thru 8. $45; 9 and 10. $35.

Watkins-Pitchford, D.J.
1. $100; 2 thru 6. $85; 7 thru 28. $75; 29 thru 43. $65; 44 thru 46. $50.

Watson, Clyde
1. $45; 2 thru 5. $35.

Watson, Colin
1. $65; 2 thru 8. $55; 9 thru 16. $45.

Watson, Ian
1. $35; 2 thru 9. $25; 10 and 11. 20.

Watts, Peter
1. $40; 2 thru 13. $30; 14 thru 75. $25; 76 thru 111. $20; 112 thru 124. $15.

Waugh, Hillary
1. $60; 2 thru 4. $45; 5 thru 13. $35; 14 thru 33. $25; 34 thru 43. $20.

Way, Margaret
1 and 2. $25; 3 thru 37. $20; 38 thru 43. $15.

Wayne, Jenifer
1. $40; 2. $30; 3 thru 11. $25; 12 thru 20. $20.

Webb, Jack
1. $60; 2 thru 16. $45; 17 thru 19. $35.

Webb, Jean Francis
1. $60; 2 and 3. $45; 4 thru 7. $40; 8 thru 22. $35; 23 thru 32. $30; 33 thru 36. $25; 37 and 38. $20.

Webster, Jean
1. $75; 2 thru 6. $50; 7. $85; 8 and 9. $50; 10. $35.

Weinbaum, Stanley G.
1. $100; 2. $85; 3 thru 6. $50; 7. $35.

Weir, Rosemary
1 and 2. $30; 3 thru 6. $25; 7 thru 43. $20.

Welch, James
1. $25; 2 and 3. $20.

Welcome, John
1. $40; 2 thru 7. $30; 8 and 9. $45; 10 thru 14. $25; 15 thru 20. $20.

Wellman, Manly Wade
1. $175; 2 thru 8. $150; 9 thru 33. $145; 34 thru 62. $140; 63. $135; 64. $125; 65. $100; 66 thru 71. $85.

Wellman, Paul I.
1. $95; 2 thru 8. $60; 9 thru 23. $50; 24. $85; 25 thru 34. $40.

Wells, Carolyn
1 and 2. $125; 3 thru 43. $90; 44 thru 84. $80; 85 thru 124. $70; 125 thru 155. $60; 156 thru 163. $50.

Wells, H.G.
1. $125; 2 thru 16. $175; 17 thru 38. $165; 39 thru 78. $150; 79. $185; 80 thru 90. $140; 91. $185; 92. $165; 93 thru 105. $140; 106. $150; 107 thru 143. $130; 144 thru 146. $100; 147 thru 153. $65; 154 and 155. $50.

Wentworth, Patricia
1 and 2. $75; 3 thru 9. $60; 10 thru 20. $55; 21 thru 55. $50; 56 thru 84. $45; 85 thru 87. $40.

Wersba, Barbara
1. $35; 2 thru 6. $25; 7 thru 11. $20.

West, Joyce
1. $65; 2. $35; 3 thru 11. $30; 12. $25.

West, Kingsley
1. $35; 2 thru 8. $25; 9. $20.

West, Tom
1. $50; 2 thru 13. $35; 14 thru 30. $30; 31 thru 47. $25; 48 thru 58. $20.

West, Wallace George
1. $45; 2 and 3. $35; 4 and 5. $30; 6. $25; 7 thru 10. $20; 11 thru 19. $15.

Westerman, Percy
1. $75; 2 thru 40. $55; 41 thru 79. $50; 80 thru 139. $45; 140 thru 176. $40.

Westlake, Donald E.
1. $75; 2 thru 36. $60; 37 thru 61. $50; 62 and 63. $45.

Weston, Carolyn
1. $35; 2 thru 5. $25; 6 and 7. $20.

Westwood, Gwen
1 and 2. $35; 3 thru 8. $25; 9 thru 17. $20; 18 and 19. $15.

Wheatley, Dennis
1 thru 3. $75; 4 thru 34. $65; 35 thru 56. $55; 57 thru 67. $45; 68 thru 76. $35.

Whitaker, Rod
1. $45; 2 thru 6. $35.

White, Eliza Orne
1. $100; 2 thru 7. $75; 8 thru 13. $65; 14 thru 17. $55; 18 thru 24. $45; 25 thru 38. $35.

White, E.B.
1. $325; 2. $150; 3 thru 10. $125; 11 and 12. $100; 13. $275; 14 thru 16. $75; 17. $40.

White, Ethel Lina
1. $45; 2. $35; 3 thru 19. $30; 20. $25; 21 thru 23. $20.

White, James
1. $45; 2 thru 10. $35; 11 thru 18. $25.

White, Jon Manchip
1. $45; 2 thru 11. $35; 12 thru 17. $30; 18 thru 25. $25.

White, Lionel
1. $55; 2 thru 17. $45; 18 thru 31. $40; 32 thru 35. $35.

White, Stewart Edward
1. $125; 2. $100; 3 thru 14. $85; 15 thru 29. $75; 30 thru 40. $65; 41 thru 55. $55; 56 thru 58. $45.

White, Ted
1. $60; 2 thru 10. $45; 11 thru 14. $35.

White, T.H.
1. $125; 2. $100; 3 thru 14. $75; 15 and 16. $65; 17 thru 22. $55; 23 and 24. $45; 25. $35.

Whitechurch, Victor L.
1. $75; 2 thru 5. $65; 6 thru 10. $55; 11 thru 22. $45; 23 thru 26. $35.

Whitfield, Raoul
1. $60; 2 thru 7. $45; 8. $35.

Whitney, Phyllis A.
1. $90; 2 thru 4. $75; 5 thru 9. $65; 10 thru 26. $55; 27 thru 49. $45; 50 thru 62. $35.

Whitson, John H.
1. $125; 2 thru 5. $85; 6 thru 22. $75; 23 thru 29. $65.

Whittington, Harry
1. $45; 2 thru 63. $35; 64 thru 104. $25; 105 thru 111. $20; 112 thru 120. $15.

Wibberley, Leonard
1. $75; 2 thru 11. $65; 12. $85; 13 thru 31. $55; 32 thru 79. $45; 80 thru 101. $35.

Wiggin, Kate Douglas
1. $165; 2. $125; 3. $100; 4 thru 13. $85; 14 and 15. $75; 16. $125; 17 thru 22. $75; 23 thru 28. $65; 29 thru 33. $55; 34. $45.

Wilcox, Collin
1. $50; 2 and 3. $45; 4 thru 17. $35.

Wilder, Laura Ingalls
1. $75; 2 thru 5. $55; 6 thru 8. $45; 9. $25.

Wilhelm, Kate
1. $65; 2. $50; 3 thru 9. $45; 10 thru 19. $35.

Willard, Barbara
1. $45; 2 thru 8. $35; 9 thru 16. $25; 17 thru 24. $20; 25 and 26. $15.

Williams, Claudette
1. $25; 2 thru 10. $20; 11 thru 14. $15.

Williams, Gordon
1. $50; 2 thru 5. $40; 6 thru 16. $35.

Williams, Jay
1. $75; 2. $65; 3 thru 7. $50; 8 thru 15. $45; 16 thru 41. $40; 42 thru 67. $35.

Williams, Jeanne
1. $50; 2 thru 4. $40; 5 thru 11. $35; 12 thru 38. $30; 39 thru 45. $25.

Williams, John
1. $50; 2. $40; 3 thru 5. $35; 6. $25.

Williams, John A.
1. $45; 2 thru 8. $35; 9. $45; 10 and 11. $25; 12. $45; 13 thru 16. $25.

Williams, Robert Moore
1. $75; 2 thru 5. $55; 6 thru 21. $45; 22 thru 28. $35.

Williams, Ursula Moray
1. $50; 2 thru 20. $45; 21 thru 34. $35; 35 thru 45. $30; 46 thru 59. $25.

Williams, Valentine
1. $85; 2 thru 5. $65; 6 thru 17. $55; 18 thru 36. $45; 37. $35.

Williamson, Jack
1. $125; 2. $85; 3 thru 5. $75; 6 thru 16. $65; 17 thru 28. $55; 29 thru 36. $45; 37. $35.

Willis, Ted
1. $50; 2 thru 9. $40; 10 thru 15. $35; 16 thru 25. $25.

Wills, Cecil M.
1. $75; 2 thru 12. $60; 13 thru 25. $45; 26 and 27. $35.

Wilson, Barbara Ker
1. $45; 2 and 3. $35; 4 thru 15. $30; 16 thru 19. $25.

Wilson, Colin
1. $50; 2 thru 4. $45; 5 thru 26. $40; 27 thru 51. $35.

Wilson, Harry Leon
1. $175; 2 thru 7. $100; 8. $125; 9 thru 11. $75; 12. $100; 13. $75; 14. $125; 15 thru 20. $75; 21. $55.

Wilson, Richard
1. $50; 2. $40; 3 thru 5. $35.

Wilson, Robert Anton
1. $50; 2 thru 5. $35.

Winsor, Kathleen
1. $100; 2. $85; 3. $65; 4. $45; 5. $25; 6. $20.

Winspear, Violet
1. $30; 2 thru 22. $20; 23 thru 58. $15; 59 thru 61. $10.

Winston, Daoma
1. $35; 2 thru 15. $30; 16 thru 46. $25; 47 thru 49. $20.

Winther, Sophus K.
1. $45; 2 thru 5. $35; 6. $25.

Wister, Owen
1. $325; 2. $175; 3 and 4. $225; 5 and 6. $175; 7. $275; 8 thru 13. $175; 14 and 15. $150; 16 thru 20. $125; 21. $45; 22. $35.

Witting, Clifford
1. $65; 2 thru 5. $50; 6 thru 9. $45; 10 thru 13. $40; 14 thru 17. $35; 18 and 19. $35.

Wolfe, Gene
1. $60; 2 thru 4. $45; 5 thru 8. $35.

Wollheim, Donald A.
1. $125; 2 thru 5. $60; 6 thru 8. $50; 9. $45.

Wood, Lorna
1. $65; 2 thru 4. $60; 5. $55; 6 thru 14. $45; 15 thru 17. $40; 18 thru 21. $35.

Woodiwiss, Kathleen E.
1. $50; 2. $40; 3 and 4. $35.

Woods, Sara
1. $50; 2 thru 16. $40; 17 thru 30. $35.

Woolf, Douglas
1. $50; 2 thru 4. $40; 5 thru 9. $35.

Woolrich, Cornell
1. $325; 2. $250; 3 thru 16. $225; 17 thru 26. $200; 27 thru 44. $175; 45 thru 48. $150; 49. $85; 50. $65.

Worboys, Anne
1. $45; 2 thru 13. $35; 14 thru 28. $30; 29 and 30. $25.

Wormser, Richard
1. $65; 2 thru 5. $45; 6 thru 11. $35; 12 thru 31. $30; 32 thru 40. $25.

Wren, P.C.
1. $125; 2 thru 8. $65; 9 thru 17. $55; 18 thru 45. $45; 46 and 47. $35.

Wright, Austin Tappan
1. $225.

Wright, Harold Bell
1. $125; 2 and 3. $100; 4 thru 9. $85; 10 thru 14. $75; 15 thru 19. $65.

Wright, S. Fowler
1. $85; 2 thru 11. $65; 12 thru 52. $55; 53 thru 62. $45.

Wrightson, Patricia
1. $45; 2. $35; 3 thru 7. $30; 8 thru 10. $25.

Wylie, Philip
1. $100; 2. $85; 3 thru 7. $75; 8. $165; 9. $150; 10 thru 25. $75; 26 thru 36. $55; 37 thru 42. $45; 43 thru 45. $35.

Wynd, Oswald
1. $85; 2 thru 5. $65; 6 thru 8. $55; 9 thru 21. $45; 22 thru 32. $35.

Wyndham, John
1. $125; 2 thru 4. $65; 5. $100; 6. $85; 7 thru 14. $55; 15. $75; 16. $55; 17 thru 21. $45; 22 thru 27. $35.

Wyndham, Lee
1. $45; 2 thru 21. $35; 22 thru 37. $30; 38 thru 41. $25.

Wynne, May
1. $100; 2 thru 19. $75; 20 thru 76. $65; 77 thru 139. $55; 140 thru 194. $45; 195 thru 207. $35.

Yarbro, Chelsea Quinn
1. $60; 2 thru 8. $45; 9 thru 15. $35.

Yates, A.G.
1. $65; 2 thru 35. $45; 36 thru 38. $35.

Yates, Dornford
1. $65; 2 thru 14. $50; 15 thru 28. $45; 29 thru 39. $35.

Yates, Elizabeth
1. $60; 2 thru 9. $45; 10 thru 28. $35; 29 thru 42. $30; 43 thru 48. $25.

Yerby, Frank
1. $75; 2 thru 4. $55; 5 thru 15. $50; 16 thru 23. $45; 24 thru 31. $40; 32. $35.

Yolen, Jane
1. $35; 2 thru 14. $30; 15 thru 38. $25.

Yorke, Margaret
1. $45; 2 and 3. $35; 4 thru 11. $30; 12 thru 22. $25.

Young, Delbert Alton
1. $35; 2 and 3. $25; 4 and 5. $20.

Young, Gordon
1. $65; 2 thru 12. $50; 13 thru 27. $45; 28 thru 42. $35.

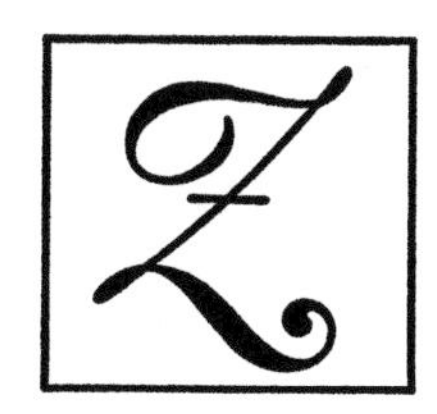

Zagat, Arthur Leo
1. $75.

Zangwill, Israel
1. $325; 2. $250; 3 thru 6. $225; 7. $250; 8 thru 20. $225; 21 thru 34. $200; 35 thru 50. $175; 51 thru 59. $150; 60. $75; 61. $65.

Zebrowski, George
1. $35; 2 and 3. $25; 4 and 5. $20.

Zelazny, Roger
1. $65; 2 thru 8. $50; 9 thru 25. $45; 26 and 27. $35.

Zinberg, Len
1. $60; 2 thru 4. $45; 5 thru 21. $40; 22 thru 39. $35.

Zindel, Paul
1. $60; 2. $45; 3. $40; 4 thru 6. $35.

Zion, Gene
1. $35; 2 thru 10. $30; 11 thru 14. $25.

Zolotow, Charlotte
1. $65; 2. $50; 3 thru 13. $45; 14 thru 43. $40; 44 thru 57. $35.

ORDER FORM

The Collector's Bookshelf

The Collector's Bookshelf can be obtained from your book-dealer or directly from Prometheus Books.

Please enclose $69.95 plus $2.00 postage and handling. Prices are subject to change without notice.

Send to ____

(Please type or print clearly)

Address ____

City ____________________ State ________ Zip ______________

Amount enclosed ______________

Charge my ☐ **VISA** ☐ **MasterCard**

Account # | | | | | | | | | | | | | | | | |

Exp. Date ______ / ______ Tel. ____________________

Signature ____

Prometheus Books

59 John Glenn Dr., Amherst, New York 14228

Phone orders call toll free: (800) 421-0351

Please allow 3-6 weeks for delivery